FOR
HANS ULI

by
KATHLEEN M. DUNCAN

LONDON
PICKERING & INGLIS LTD.
1971

PICKERING & INGLIS LTD.
29 LUDGATE HILL, LONDON, E.C.4
26 BOTHWELL STREET, GLASGOW, C.2

Printed in Great Britain by A. McLay & Co. Ltd., Cardiff

For Alex and Gillian

A Fountain and a Friend

1 SOMEWHERE A DOOR BANGED. STARTLED
out of sleep, Simon sat up, certain that he was still dreaming.
He blinked at the unfamiliar room, with its bare polished
floor. The great puffy warm mound on his feet was quite
unlike his own blue eiderdown.

Then he caught sight of his suitcase and he remembered.
Of course! This was Switzerland!

A great tide of excitement surged up inside him as he tried
to sort out jumbled memories of the day before. First the
airport near London and the long wait with Uncle Max
because the plane was delayed somewhere. Then a terribly
late start more than three hours after the trip should have
begun.

Simon remembered the thrill of being in the air, but he
couldn't recall travelling in the train from Basle. It had been
quite dark when they reached there, and he must have fallen
asleep.

One, two, three, four, five, six, seven. A clock struck with
a slow booming note outside the open window. Simon threw
off the puffy feather coverlet and ran to look out.

Opposite his window was a mountain—a dark green
mountain, with fir trees growing on it right up into the sky.
And there, with the morning sun on its face, was a church
clock with the hands standing at seven. The air was sparkling
clear, and somewhere a cuckoo was calling.

It took Simon about three minutes to get dressed. There
was a handbasin with a queer kind of spout in it, and a
mirror too high up for him to see himself, so he didn't
trouble about washing.

In between pulling on his jersey and trying to find his

socks he ran to look out of the window again. Swifts were swooping and screaming past it, and he could also hear somebody whistling.

This time he looked down, instead of up at the mountain. To his surprise Uncle Max was in the yard below doing something to a small blue car.

"Hi!" called Simon, and Uncle Max looked up.

"Hi!" he answered. "I thought you were going to sleep the clock round. You just didn't want to know anything after we left the plane last night. Hurry and come down, it's a pity to waste any of a day like this."

"I'm coming now, when I've put on my socks. How do I get out to you? I don't know this house."

"It's a hotel, remember. A lot of people in it aren't awake yet, so come quietly. Just keep on coming down the stairs and you'll find the door."

In all Simon's nine years he had never been so excited. This was really Switzerland, where Grandmother lived, and where Uncle Max had had all sorts of adventures in the mountains.

He opened his door softly and stepped out on to a strange kind of matting, quite different from the faded staircarpet at home. Everything smelt different too, a clean scent of soap and polish and pine woods, and a lovely fragrance of coffee was added to it.

Once downstairs he paused to look at an enormous carved bear which held a hatrack, and then he found the front door. It stood wide open, and Simon slipped out into the sunshine.

There was no sign of Uncle Max or the car. Just chestnut trees shading little red tables and chairs, and a fishpond with a fountain in it. But the sound of whistling led him round the corner, and there was the yard he had seen from his window.

"Hullo!" said Uncle Max, straightening up, and closing the bonnet of the car. "So you found your way. What do you want to do now?"

"Explore! That's a whopping mountain behind the church, can I go up it?"

"Not before breakfast. I suggest you go and see how quickly you can find a fountain, but don't cross the road and come back on the same pavement. This little town can be quite busy early in the morning. You can see the church clock from every street here, watch it, and be back in fifteen minutes."

Joyfully, Simon found the narrow street, and looked left and right. Which way should he go? He knew he could not get lost if he kept on the same pavement, but pavements go both ways, and which way would a fountain be?

He suddenly remembered the fountain in the little fishpond right behind him. Had Uncle Max been teasing? Surely not, because he had been so special about fifteen minutes. There must be another fountain somewhere.

In any case the houses themselves made Simon want to stand and stare. Some were tall and old, with balconies and shutters to every window, but others were low and wide with carving on their eaves.

They had deep verandahs with flower boxes on them, and they looked just like the musical box Grandmother had sent him for Christmas. But these were real houses and had people living in them.

He went slowly along, glancing into the small shops, and then some swallows swooped so low above his head that he looked up. He stood still, gazing in wonder. Right opposite him, high above the Post Office, was a great shining range of mountains.

They were not green like the one outside his bedroom window, but dazzling snowy peaks with blue shadows on them, as blue as the sky.

People went by him on their way to work but they did not look surprised to see Simon standing there. A man in bright blue overalls smiled, and stopped. "Jungfrau!" he said, pointing above the Post Office roof, but Simon didn't understand him, so he hurried on.

At last Simon went on too, gazing back over his shoulder at every few steps, and because he wasn't looking where he was going he didn't see someone coming in the opposite direction. A terrific bump knocked him off his feet.

He hit the cobbled pavement very hard indeed, and so did the other boy, whose schoolbooks scattered into the roadway.

"Pardon! I run too fast and do not see."

"I—I'm sorry—I wasn't looking either," stammered Simon, sitting up and rubbing his elbow to ease the bruise.

The other boy scrambled to his feet. He was a little taller than Simon, and wore a yellow shirt and leather shorts. On his feet were very stout hobnailed boots, and his satchel was strapped across his back.

"You speak English!" Simon exclaimed as the boy helped him up with a friendly jerk.

"We learn at school, and my father speaks well," the boy explained. "You have a holiday?' You are staying here?"

"At the little hotel under the mountain back there," Simon told him, and the boy nodded "I know it. The porter, Peter, is my good friend."

"How old are you?" cried Simon, "What's your name? Could I play with you sometimes?"

"I have eleven years and my name is Hans Uli, but I must go to school. Perhaps I will find you when school is over. Where do you go now?"

While he picked up his books and settled them under his arm again Simon told him about the fountain.

"Uncle Max sent me to see how quickly I could find one," he explained.

Hans Uli laughed, and waved towards the street corner just beyond them. "One there" he said, "one at our school—one by the bridge, they are everywhere!"

"But why?" asked Simon.

Hans Uli shrugged his shoulders. "Much water comes from the mountains," he said, as though that explained everything.

Then he stepped back to the corner that he had just come round so fast, and took a look up at the church clock. "It is nearly schooltime already," he said, with a guilty look, "I have to run!"

"But it's too early," protested Simon, not anxious to lose his new friend.

"No, it will be too late," Hans Uli assured him. "When I was small I was there at nine o'clock. Now I must be there at eight, and when I have grown some more it will be half past seven. I will find you," he added cheerfully, and went off very fast, his heavy boots clattering as he ran.

Simon was enormously happy that he had found a friend. He turned the corner and saw a wide cobbled square with very old houses all round it. Right opposite him was the church, and the clock on the tower said twenty minutes to eight. "Only five minutes left," he thought regretfully, but it didn't matter, for in the middle of the square was a fountain.

Red geraniums bloomed at each side of it, and on the top was a statue of a little girl holding a shell. The water that poured from it into the basin was sparkling clear, and two sparrows bathed in a little puddle near the rim.

Simon wished that he had a camera with a colour film in it so that he could keep that bright picture always. "I guess there's a postcard of that in one of the shops," he thought, and planned to buy one and send it home to Mother. Some children came across the square laughing and talking, girls as well as boys. One or two wore bright red and green aprons which made them look unlike English children. Simon's happiness clouded a little as he saw them. He remembered Philippa.

When grandmother had invited him to come to Switzerland with Uncle Max, because Mother was busy with the new baby, she had invited her other grandchild too. Philippa was Aunt Jean's little girl, but Simon had never met her.

"Simon is nine, and Philippa is eight," Grandmother had written, "so if Max brings Simon out on his next business trip they should be good companions for each other."

Simon wasn't at all sure about that. If Philippa had been a boy it would have been different, but a girl could just about spoil the holiday for him, he decided. Also he loved Grandmother very much, and when she came to stay with them in England they had wonderful times together. Now he would have a rival for her attention, and it didn't please him.

"She'll probably be soppy and spoilt," he thought gloomily, and was very glad that he had met Hans Uli. Suddenly he wished very much that Uncle Max could stay with them, instead of driving off in that little blue car to get on with his business, which was something to do with those worrying words "Exports and Imports".

Thinking of Uncle Max made him glance at the clock. He was nearly late already. He raced back the way he had come, forgetting about Philippa in his anxiety not to be in disgrace on that first lovely morning. Uncle Max had said "not before breakfast" when he had asked about going up the mountain, would he say "yes" later in the day?

Simon fervently hoped so, and determined to be on his very best behaviour.

He arrived panting under the chestnut trees in front of the hotel, skirted round the red tables and chairs, and nearly fell over a small figure kneeling by the pool. With her arm deep in the water the little girl had not heard him coming. She looked up with a start, and sat back on her heels, pushing her black hair out of her eyes with a wet hand.

"Hullo!" she said, "I'm Philippa. I'm trying to see if the goldfish will nibble my fingers. You try it, they might like the taste of yours, and breakfast isn't nearly ready yet."

by where I think you may play. You will like the river too, as long as you promise not to get too near the edge. It's very deep, and freezing cold I'm sure."

"Have you ever heard of a boy called Hans Uli about here, Mother?" asked Uncle Max, helping himself to his third cup of coffee, "Simon met him this morning, and he assures me that Peter the porter knows him. He might make a good playmate after school."

"Hans Uli. Why, yes I know him, he's a very nice boy. His father is employed by Alexis Stahel."

"Is he indeed!" Uncle Max raised his eyebrows and looked impressed.

"I never thought of him as a playmate for Simon because he is older," said grandmother, thoughtfully, "but that seems to have settled itself as they have met. Hans Uli has a younger sister, too, I believe, as well as Helga. Helga has been a wonderful little mother to the family since poor Klaus lost his wife. I shall be very happy if these two can be with them sometimes."

"Good!" said Simon fervently, and leaned back in his chair with a sigh of content. Uncle Max tucked his napkin away in its little green case, and showed Philippa how to fold hers. "Now I'm away," he said, as he helped his mother up. "Have a good day you two, and don't get lost."

But they didn't have a chance to get lost that morning, because Grandmother had arranged a treat for them. Fortunately, it was one which she could enjoy as well, and Simon just hoped that he would be allowed to climb the green mountain another day.

"Stay close by," she told them, after Uncle Max had gone, "I shall want you both in a little while, so don't get too untidy."

"What will she want us for?" Simon asked Philippa, as Grandmother, after a friendly little chat with the head waitress, went limping away towards her room. "I don't know. But we'll go and play Dab on one of those red tables under the trees till we're called." Philippa led the way, quite certain that Simon would agree to whatever she wanted to do. She had wondered what it would be like to have a boy cousin to play with, because she had only two baby sisters, and she was finding it very jolly indeed.

"What's 'dab'!" asked Simon, suspiciously.

"I'll show you. It's terribly easy, but . . . " Philippa stopped, and ran towards the pavement. "Look!" she cried. Look! Here's a horse coming with a green carriage. It's got red wheels to it. Let's go and get Grandma so that she can see. Grandma, Grandma! Come quickly!"

The little green carriage came slowly up the street, and the horse, which was black and white, seemed in no hurry at all. Simon stood and watched it, wishing it would stop.

Philippa had gone racing away, and she met her grandmother in the hall.

"Come quickly! quickly!" she urged. "There's a lovely horse and carriage . . . "

To her surprise the old lady seemed quite calm. "Ah! Mr. Berg," she said, "he has arrived then. He is always just on time, never late. Will you run out and tell him that I will be ready in a moment."

"Tell the man—with the horse? Does he know you?"

"We are old friends," said grandmother, and she reached a light grey cloak down from the hatrack that the carved bear held. She did not trouble about a hat, but tucked her shabby old handbag under her arm and hobbled to the door.

Five minutes later they were all jogging steadily out of the old town, and across the wide bridge to the newer town with its fine shops on the other side of the river. The clip clop of the black and white horse was a wonderful slow way of travelling to the children, who were used to the speed of their fathers' cars.

"I can see all round and see everything properly. I LOVE this green carriage," said Philippa, busy imagining herself a royal personage.

Simon was too happy to talk much. He was so afraid that he might miss something beautiful, or exciting, if he talked. He saw four fountains with their clear water splashing into old stone troughs, and everywhere there were flowers. On balconies, in tubs on pavements, and in little boxes by shop doors. Every time that he looked up at the houses and shops he saw the mountains beyond them, with sunshine glittering on the snow, and he longed to go climbing right up there as Uncle Max had done.

"Are they very far away, Grandma?" he asked.

"The mountains? No, only a car drive, and then a long walk. One day I'm sure you will see them closer than this. Perhaps I could get someone to take you. We shall see."

Only a car drive! "How long a car drive?" Simon wanted to know, but Grandmother wasn't listening. She was speaking to Mr. Berg, and she was speaking German very fast. Simon and Philippa looked at each other, and Philippa giggled. "What's so funny?" asked the old lady, quite sharply.

"I didn't mean to be rude, but it sounds just like—like gargling," Philippa explained, flushing, and suppressing her giggles.

"One day I'll learn to speak it too," decided Simon, as Mr. Berg brought the carriage to a standstill.

"We get out here," Grandmother told them briskly. "There are some shops I think you will like to see. Mr. Berg is meeting us later."

Philippa was delighted at the idea of looking at shops, but Simon's heart sank. 'Girls' stuff' he thought dismally, and determined to stand outside looking at the mountains. He hated waiting about while his mother did the shopping at home. It was too bad to have to do it on a holiday.

But as they followed Grandmother's tapping stick along the pavement he found that she was leading them to quite a different kind of shop from any he knew at home. It was full of wooden animals, beautifully carved. "Oh! Look at those bears. And a little bear with cubs—and goats! Grandma, there's a chalet too, like you sent for Christmas."

For ten minutes they stood absorbed, and Simon wanted one of those fierce looking bears more than anything in the world.

Philippa sighed for a cuckoo clock. They were there in all sizes, with their pendulums wagging away at a tremendous rate. But Grandmother was not buying any presents that day.

"Look at everything," she said, "and we'll come to the shop again before you go home. By then you will have decided what you really want. In any case, there are so many other shops which sell carvings that you may find something you like better."

With difficulty they dragged themselves away, and Simon found that there were things for boys as well as girls in the shop next door.

He saw bright red braces with flowers embroidered on them which were just as gay as the fine Swiss blouses. Philippa was wild to possess one of those, but Grandmother would not promise.

"What are the flowers?" Philippa wanted to know. "The same ones are embroidered on everything. I can see forget-me-nots, and some yellow ones like cowslips, but the big blue ones and the white ones don't grow in our garden."

"The blue are gentians, and the white are edelweiss. Those are flowers of the high alps, and the edelweiss grows in such dangerous places that only true mountaineers see it growing wild I think. The Swiss love it as their national flower, just as we say 'the rose of England'."

'Edelweiss—Edelweiss' the name went through Simon's head like a song, and he glanced up at the great white peaks and imagined it growing where those blue shadows were.

"One day I'll climb," he said, almost under his breath, but Philippa heard. "I will too then," she declared, "and I'll get higher than you."

"Climbing is for men," retorted Simon, scornfully.

"It is for both," his grandmother told him calmly. "Women climb splendidly, though I admit that an accident years ago helped to make me lame in my old age. I think if you two are going to argue I had better find a cafe, and keep you busy eating."

"Did YOU climb?" both children looked at her with astonished eyes.

"I managed the Matterhorn once," she answered dryly, and led them into a sunny courtyard where there were tables under orange coloured sunshades. They chose one where they could sit in the shade and watch the busy street. Other carriages like Mr. Berg's, with visitors in them, trotted by among the glossy motor-cars.

"Swiss pastries are wonderful," Grandmother told them, "but I dare you to be sick. Do both of you like cream?"

"Oooooo!" Simon left her in no doubt, and Philippa murmured blissfully, "It's a long, long time till lunch."

"Poor Hans Uli having to be in school today," said Simon a few minutes later, through a mouthful of chocolate eclair.

Grandmother was enjoying his enjoyment so much that she forgot to tell him about talking with his mouth full. "I don't think Hans Uli would envy you," she said, "though he might like a holiday from school. This side of the river is very much a holiday world for visitors, with all the big shops and hotels. He is a country boy really, he loves the animals and the little meadows, as I do. He finds his fun fishing, and walking in the hills."

"There's Mr. Berg with his carriage on the other side of the street—can I take some sugars for his horse?"

Philippa slipped from her chair and ran to watch the green carriage turning round. She loved the holiday world of shops and cream cakes, but she liked the little green carriage best of all.

The black and white horse, whose name was Eiger, accepted lumps of sugar gently from her flattened palm, while Mr. Berg helped Grandmother to her seat.

"Has it been a nice morning?" she asked, as they trotted slowly to the bridge.

"A gorgeous morning," answered Philippa, with a sigh of content.

"But I like the old town best," decided Simon, as they reached the cobbled squares again. Suddenly he remembered the fountain that he had first seen that morning. "Will there be picture postcards like we have at home?" he asked, as they watched Mr. Berg drive away from the hotel.

"Of course, plenty at the little Post Office down the street. Do you want some to send home?"

"I do. I want some with flowers on them for Mummy," cried Philippa. "Be careful how you cross then," Grandmother told them, and counted out some money from her purse. "Ask how much they are," she said, "and look at the change, so that you can see what the different coins are. Don't forget that you'll need some stamps as well."

Leaning on her stick she watched them as they raced away to do their first shopping with foreign money.

The Post Office had a counter, like a stall, facing the street. On it were racks of coloured postcards with pictures of mountains, and lakes, and one of some little boys in gay costumes.

Philippa was delighted with that one, but puzzled about the immensely long tube with a wide end which one of them was holding.

"I like the boys, and the flowers round them," she said to Simon, "but I don't know what that queer thing is."

A jolly looking man who was choosing postcards further down the counter turned and smiled. "That's an alpenhorn," he told them. "People who live high up in the mountains have them, they blow down the narrow end and a lovely sound comes out—when it's done properly, that is!"

"Like a trumpet?" suggested Simon.

"Like a trumpet far away," replied the man. "Once you

have heard it echoing across the valleys you will never forget it."

He turned away to get stamps from a machine, and choosing four cards between them, Simon and Philippa showed the smiling person behind the counter the money they had been given.

"You want stamps?" she asked, and showed them which coins to put in the slot.

"I like it here, it's a good sort of Post Office," said Simon, sticking the stamps on his cards right away in case he dropped them. The jolly man was just going to walk away towards the square, but he stopped a moment to ask if they had seen the big main Post Office across the bridge.

"We've been across in the big town this morning, with Mr. Berg," said Philippa, "and we saw lots of carved bears, but not a Post Office. Is it special?"

"I think it's the only one I know in the middle of a town which has a duck-pond in front of it," answered the man with a chuckle. "Don't forget to go and look before your holiday is over."

"A duck-pond!" cried Simon, thinking of the rather muddy one not far from his home where he liked to fish for frog spawn. "Don't the ducks get run over by the cars and things?"

"Oh, they can't do that. It's a very special pond with sparkling clear water, and the ducks are Mandarins—those splendid coloured fellows that look like toys. They have little houses hidden among the flowers on the bank. I think their wings are clipped so that they don't fly. But only a very silly duck would want to fly away from there."

He raised his hat to Philippa, to her great pleasure and surprise, and walked off down the street.

"He was nice," said Simon, "it's all nice here. Only a VERY nice place would have ducks at the Post Office. Suppose Grandmother hadn't asked us to come and stay, wouldn't that have been AWFUL!"

Philippa looked thoughtful. "I guess we ought to buy Grandma a present," she said. "It's a way of saying 'thank you for having us' Mummy told me."

Simon nodded. "We'll spend our Saturday money on it," he said, "and we'll spend it here."

The Chalet with Bells

3 PETER THE PORTER WAS FREE FOR SOME time after lunch had finished. He came into the little yard with his accordion and tried to show the children how to play it.

He was a fat, jolly man, and he could play fast and wonderful tunes which ended with a great flourish. When Simon tried terrible groans came from the instrument, and Philippa only managed three notes in succession.

They laughed so much that Peter had to sit down on a bench and mop his forehead with a bright blue handkerchief.

They were still there in the drowsy heat of the afternoon when Hans Uli came round the corner. Simon sprang up, delighted to see him again, and that he had kept his promise.

"You're early! That's smashing!" he cried, "Come and listen to Peter—he knows some super tunes."

"Hans Uli and Peter already are friends," said the porter, his round face creasing in a smile. "I think school is quick today, and Hans Uli has perhaps been running."

Hans Uli laughed and picked up the accordion. Putting the strap over his shoulder he played a gentle little tune which impressed Simon enormously.

"I don't think I could ever do that," he said, feeling envious.

"One day perhaps," answered Hans Uli. "I have eleven years you see, and you are not so old. Peter makes me learn well."

He spoke to Peter in German, even faster than Mr. Berg.

"Hans Uli wishes you to go to his home," explained the porter, turning to Simon, "I think that Madam your grandmother should be asked, yes?"

"I'll go," cried Philippa, and dashed indoors, quite sure that she was included in the invitation.

"Can she come?" asked Simon anxiously, "I mean—do you mind girls?"

"But no! I have two sisters and they are not very terrible. Sometimes they talk too much, but my small sister Kati, she will play I think with—what—how are you called?"

"How are we what? Oh! names you mean! I'm Simon, and she's Philippa. She's my cousin, not my sister. My mother has a new baby, but he's a boy, which is a jolly good thing."

"Undoubtedly," said Peter, and they all looked very wise.

Two minutes later Philippa came flying back. In that brief time she had put on a clean dress and brushed her hair. They could go to Hans Uli's house, she said, but they were to be home not a minute later than six.

"We can watch the church clock," said Simon.

"We have a better clock at home," Hans Uli told him, and his grey eyes twinkled as Peter winked at him.

It was only a very short way to Hans Uli's home. Just down two narrow side streets, where the sun could hardly touch the yellow pansies in the window boxes, and then they came to a wider road which seemed to lead straight to the green mountain.

Right on the corner was a very old chalet. It was small, and its wooden walls were dark with age. The long balconies were so close under the deep eaves that Simon thought it looked rather like a ship with an upper and lower deck. Half of the lower part of the house was filled with great logs, and trunks of trees, and a wooden stairway led up to the balcony.

Hans Uli pushed open the gate of a small neat garden, and beckoned them in. "This is home," he said proudly.

"It's like a fairy-tale house," cried Philippa, "I didn't know that real ones could ever be like this . . . "

"It is old," Hans Uli told them, and he pointed to a long band of carved letters on the edge of the balcony.

"I can see '1720' at the end of the writing, but what do the words say?" asked Simon.

"God bless all who shall live in this house. Built by Hans and Klaus Werner. 1720" translated Hans Uli. "That is what you call many grandfathers ago."

"Ancestors," corrected Simon, "It's super. Is your name Werner too?"

Hans Uli nodded. "My father is Klaus Werner, there is always a Klaus or a Hans in our family."

"And does God bless you specially, because you live in that house?" asked Philippa with interest.

Hans Uli shrugged his shoulders. "Perhaps," he said, "sometimes. I do not think about it. My father goes to church, and my sisters, but not me—if I can help it. I do not trouble to think about such things."

Simon didn't answer, but he felt a bit unhappy about Hans Uli's answer, and Philippa, though she didn't say so, was shocked. Sunday was such a happy day at home because they all went to church together, and there was Children's Church, which she enjoyed, while the grown-ups had their service.

"Here is my sister," said Hans Uli, changing the subject. Someone was looking down at them from the balcony. First she frowned, and then smiled, as Hans Uli spoke to her quickly in their own language.

"Helga says to come in," he said, pointing to the broad wooden stairs, and the tall girl who was so like him came to meet them.

"You are welcome. You stay in the little hotel? You know Peter? Then we are good friends!" Helga spoke English quite as well as her brother did, and she was always glad to have English people to practise it with. She worked for part of each day helping to cook in another small hotel nearer to the bridge, and then was busy keeping their own home neat, and trying to take her mother's place.

One of her worries was that Hans Uli seemed such a

solitary boy. He did not go to play with other youngsters much, and she was glad that he had brought two children home for once.

"Our little sister will like to meet you," she said, "she learns English too. Come up and find her."

Simon and Philippa pattered up in their light sandals, and Hans Uli followed in his heavy boots. The handrail was warm to touch where the sun had been all day, and at the top they found some chairs and a stout wooden table. A tortoise-shell cat slept on the broad ledge of the balcony between the flower pots.

Philippa was fascinated by the tiny windows with their heavy shutters, and the long, curiously shaped broom which leaned by the open door. Hans Uli's home reminded her of the gingerbread house in her old picture book of Hansel and Gretel.

Something else had caught Simon's attention, and he stood staring while Helga and her brother disappeared indoors. All along the wooden wall above the windows, and close under those massive eaves, were bells. A whole row of them in all sizes.

The biggest one was as big as the football he had at home, and the smallest at the end of the line no bigger than an egg-cup. Each one hung from a leather strap, and to Simon it seemed as though they must be as old as the house.

"Who would want so many bells?" he wondered. "Perhaps they used to ring them, like handbells, I'd love to try."

Philippa kneeled on a chair in the sun and stroked the tortoise-shell cat. "I expect it's difficult, like the accordion," she said.

Helga came out on to the balcony with a tray, and Hans Uli followed, pushing his small sister in front of him.

"This is Kati. She has seven years, and she learns to help Helga."

He saw Simon looking up at the bells and added proudly, "Those are from our cows and goats when Grandfather had fields, but now houses are built where it was green."

"Do cows wear them?" asked Simon astonished.

"They ring all the time as they move," explained Helga, pouring milk from a big jug into five glasses. "One can hear them if they stray when they go to the mountains. Will you take milk with us?"

She held out a glass to Philippa, and a brimming one to Simon.

"This is just for after school—tonight we eat late when our father comes home."

There was a wooden board on the tray, with a knife and cheese of various kinds, and small biscuits. Philippa said 'no thank you' because she didn't like cheese, but Simon, not wanting to be different from Hans Uli, cut himself a wedge and found that it was good.

"Made from goat's milk," said Helga, looking pleased.

The boys were very glad that Kati and Philippa soon ran away into the house. The small girls could not speak each other's language but seemed to understand about such things as dolls and dresses just the same.

Hans Uli poured himself the last drop of the milk. "Will you help me?" he asked. "I must go and turn the hay. Peter has cut it for us yesterday and now I must see that it becomes —gets—is that right?—gets dry . . . "

"Hay," cried Simon. "Have you a field then? What's it for?"

He followed as Hans Uli clattered downstairs, went round beside the woodpile and found himself a rake. "One for you," he said, handing it to Simon, and reaching down another from a hook by the backdoor.

"We have no fields now," he explained, "only a yard, but the hay is for my rabbits because the winter is very long."

He led Simon round to the other side of the house, and there, tucked under the balcony against the wall, was a row of wooden hutches. Each one housed a fine black and white

rabbit, and they stood up on their hind legs and expected
to be petted when they saw the boys.

"See how great they are," said Hans Uli, undoing the
first hutch. He lifted out a large bright-eyed one with long
black ears. The rabbit cuddled into his arms, but was quite
placid when he handed it to Simon.

Dropping the rake Simon took it carefully, delighted as
he felt the creature's softness, and because it seemed happy
to be stroked.

"Wouldn't I like a rabbit!" he sighed enviously. "We've
got guinea pigs at home, but this is nicer."

"One cannot eat guinea pigs," said the older boy in a
matter of fact voice, and Simon realised that, like his grandfather, Hans Uli was a farmer in a very small way. Only the
big rabbit he held was truly a pet.

They took it with them to a small yard which had
an apple tree in it. It was laden with blossom, and
the cut grass, warm in the sun, smelt very sweet.
The rabbit lolloped happily about, and the boys set to
work.

Simon thought he had never enjoyed anything so much
as tossing that hay. They pelted each other with it a good
deal, and made mounds, and knocked them down. Indoors
they could hear Philippa and Kati laughing as though they
were enjoying themselves too. Helga came out on the balcony,
which ran right round the house, and hung a row of washing
on a line strung under the eaves.

"Don't tread on it too much," she called down, "you
will make bad hay, and Father will be cross."

Hans Uli answered something in German which Simon
guessed was not polite, and Helga made a face. "You are a
bad boy," she retorted, but she smiled.

"Can you come with me tomorrow?" asked Hans Uli,
when she had gone indoors again. "After school I shall take
my camera and search for—and search for . . . " he stopped
with a little frown, trying to find the right word.

"A good picture?" suggested Simon, "Philippa's father does that, he's a photographer."

"A good picture, yes, but more than good. One that someone else shall not see—do you understand?"

"I think I do." Simon leaned on his rake and wished that he really knew what Hans Uli wanted. "What do you want it for? Why is it special?" he asked, in an effort to find out.

"Special! That's the word! Special for my school. Each school will send photographs to the—to the—"

"Competition—Exhibition—Art Gallery?" Simon thought of some of the words he had heard Daddy and Uncle Max use, and he knew that there were photographs at their own school Exhibition sometimes.

Hans Uli nodded. "One of those words is right," he said, "and you see I MUST make the best photograph, I MUST win for my school—then everyone will be proud and say 'Hans Uli has done it!' "

"I'll come," Simon promised eagerly. "Will you take pictures of those white mountains?"

"Of Jungfrau? Oh NO!" Hans Uli's voice was full of scorn. "Everyone takes Jungfrau—all the postcards you will see, and the lakes too. I want a small, good thing. Something as you said, special."

He drew the last of the hay into a tidy pile and went to put the rake away. "Tomorrow I will spread it again before school" he explained, "and it will get still more dry."

"Why must you take the best photo?" Simon asked, trailing after him. "Suppose someone else does?"

"If someone else does it will be Johannes," answered Hans Uli darkly, "Johannes does everything well. He is big, and his head is bigger, but he wins because he is clever. I am not clever," he explained, "school work is too difficult. I like better to be out of doors, but if I take the best picture my father will be happy."

Simon signed. He himself was not very good at spelling, or history, or geography either, so he knew just how Hans

Uli felt. His own school reports often had the uncomfortably truthful words 'Could do better'.

"We're sure to find something if we really look" he said hopefully, and wished that there was a competition at his own school like that. If there had been he would have tried to get a picture of those wonderful mountains.

Suddenly a shout from above made them look up.

"Come quick! Come quick!" Philippa was shrieking. "The cuckoo's going to strike."

Hans Uli laughed, but Simon, who had longed to see one of the cuckoos come out in the shop full of wood-carvings, raced up the stairs.

In the cool room, where Helga sat sewing, Kati had abandoned an array of dolls and joined Philippa who stood looking at the largest cuckoo clock they had seen. The pendulum swung steadily against the wooden wall, and the hand was just jerking towards five o'clock.

"There he is!" cried Philippa with delight, as the door opened above the clock face, and the little wooden bird popped out. Cuckoo! Cuckoo! it called five times, and then the door shut, and there was only the steady ticking once again.

"It's gorgeous! I wish we had one like that—I wish it would strike again soon." Philippa stood looking at the carved flowers and vine leaves which twined about the box, and the weights which were shaped like fir cones.

"Not again till another hour," Helga told her. "My grandfather made that. He made the most beautiful clocks in the Canton, and some day it will belong to Hans Uli."

"Can he carve?" asked Simon, and when Helga laughed and said, "Why no! He cannot even finish his lessons," he understood why Hans Uli wanted so much to do something special.

"Does Hans Uli find lessons difficult?" asked Philippa, when the boys had gone out into the sun again.

Helga sighed. "He does not like working, and that is the

truth of it," she said sadly. "Only if he is out of doors is he happy. He tries to find an easy way to do everything else, and he makes many mistakes because he does not like to think about lessons."

"He doesn't like going to church either," said Philippa, arranging Helga's cotton reels in a pattern on the table.

"How do you know?" asked Helga, sharply.

"He said so—just now, when we wanted to know what the words were along the balcony," answered Philippa, flushing a little. She felt that perhaps she shouldn't have said anything about church, because Helga looked unhappy.

"I hope that one day he will understand what the words on the balcony really mean. God does bless those who love Him—He blesses all men every day as well—but it is sad when one forgets to say 'thank You'."

Helga put away her sewing and went towards the kitchen.

"I begin to cook supper," she said, and Philippa decided that it must be time to go.

Something Special

4 THE NEXT DAY SEEMED A VERY LONG ONE
to Simon because he wanted it to be after-school time so
much. He wondered where Hans Uli would take him to
search for a very special thing to photograph, but there
were hours and hours to wait.

"I take you to see the river at two o'clock?" suggested
Peter, as he came to rest on the bench after carrying a lot
of suitcases for some new arrivals.

"Oh yes—please!" Simon and Philippa were delighted.
They had both wanted to be able to stand looking for a
long time at that deep green water.

Grandmother was busy with a great many letters to write,
but in the middle of the morning she came out and sat
under the chestnut trees to drink coffee. The children had
short, fat bottles of lemonade with straws, and it was very
peaceful.

"It's so quiet," said Philippa, almost in a whisper,
"except for that bird singing . . . "

"A blackbird I think . . . " began Grandmother, and then,
suddenly, it was not quiet at all. From far down the street
there came a sound they had never heard before. A clashing,
jangling, ringing sound, which grew louder. It had a shuffling,
trampling sound mixed with it.

Simon jumped up, nearly knocking the table over.

"Something's coming! It's a funny kind of band!"

"It's the cattle," said Grandmother placidly, rescuing his
lemonade bottle as it tipped.

Philippa ran out towards the pavement just as Peter,
followed by the waitresses, the chambermaids, and some of
the guests, came running from the front door.

"The cows go to the high meadows!" called Peter to the children, and he came to hold them by the hand as the first of the herd came in sight.

Even Madame Rächmi leaned out of a top window and called down to Grandmother, "It is good for the children to see, Madame!"

The noise of the bells grew tremendously loud as the slow, plodding animals passed. They were all the colour of fresh butter, with big soft brown eyes. The leaders wore the biggest bells of all on broad leather collars round their great necks. Very heavy they looked, but the cows didn't seem to mind.

After them came younger ones with smaller bells that had a different chime, and last of all the calves with tiny ones that tinkled. Men and boys were following, and a busy dog frisked round their heels. He really had no work to do just then, for the cows seemed to know exactly where they were going.

"When will they come home?" asked Philippa, anxiously.

"When the hay has been cut, and the grass has grown again down here, and it gets towards winter," Peter explained. "Have you seen Hans Uli's jacket which his uncle has given him for helping to take cows to the mountain?"

"A jacket? No! Is it a special one?" asked Philippa, and Simon felt a little pang of envy. Hans Uli might not be clever at school but he did do such exciting things.

When the last cow had disappeared along the narrow street, and everyone had gone back to work, Grandmother was still sitting resting.

"You'd better come and finish this lemonade before it gets spilled," she told them. "That was something worth seeing. It happens every spring as soon as the very high fields are clear of snow. It's lovely up there, with thousands of wild flowers, and the cows give splendid milk because the grass is so good. I wish I could get someone to take you to see it," she added with a little sigh, because her lameness prevented her from doing all kinds of nice things.

After a minute she looked happier and said, "Perhaps my friends Captain and Mrs. Yates will be coming here for a few days before you leave. They might be kind enough to include you in a tour if you promised to be good. Captain Yates wouldn't put up with any nonsense I warn you."

"Oo-oh! What a super treat!" breathed Simon, but Philippa frowned. "I'm not sure I want to go," she said, and added, "those bells were like Hans Uli has in his house—a whole long row of them."

That reminded Simon of something that Grandmother had said to Uncle Max.

"Who does Hans Uli's father work for?" he asked. "Uncle said 'does he indeed!' in a funny sort of way when you said the name."

"And well he might," Grandmother told him, pushing away her coffee cup, and settling back as though she was going to tell a story.

"Alexis Stahel is a very great man. Great in the sense that he is very wise, and works very hard."

"What does he work at?" Philippa wanted to know.

"He's a scientist. He works chiefly on medicines, but I think that, at the moment, he is busy on something that will help airmen, and the men who go exploring in space. Klaus Werner is his chauffeur and drives him to conferences in Berne, Geneva, and Paris. Professor Stahel says he likes driving himself, but if he suddenly got a good idea he might be thinking about that, and forget where he was going. He has to have Hans Uli's father to see that he gets to the right place."

"Does he live here? On this side of the bridge?"

"No, on the other side. But he has a lovely chalet high up in the mountains too, so Klaus Werner is often away from home. I think it is wonderful how young Helga manages."

"Kati helps her, and Hans Uli makes hay for the rabbits."
Philippa slipped off her chair, and went to fetch her skipping
rope from her case.

"Time I finished my letters," said Grandmother and got
up stiffly, but Simon stayed where he was, making patterns
with the chestnut blossoms which fell down on the table.
He wished he could be a scientist who helped spacemen,
and have a chalet in the mountains, but for the moment
what he most wanted was to find something special for
Hans Uli.

"I hope God blesses his photos," he thought, and frowned
a little as he wished that Hans Uli would remember to say
'thank You' for good things.

"And I must say a special big 'thank You' for this holiday
in Switzerland," he said to himself, remembering that he
had been so sleepy the night before that he had forgotten
prayers altogether.

When Peter was ready for them at two o'clock, Philippa
had borrowed some dark glasses from Grandmother because
the sun was so bright.

They set off through the square and Peter turned down
some narrow alley ways which led to the willow shaded
quay. There were plenty of small boats moored there, and
on the opposite bank they could see people fishing.

"Green water and green mountain," said Simon, for even
there they could see the dark forest which rose above the
town.

"And a blue sky and blue boats," said Philippa.

"And your red dress and my red face," chuckled Peter.
"Step carefully now, and I help you into my boat, we go
rowing for a little way."

"Oh, Peter! You never told us! Is this boat really yours?"

"Of course it is mine. See, it has my name—Peter Brun.
You must sit still, and not stand up while we go."

The seats were quite hot as he settled them side by side,
but the air felt cooler when he began to row, and pulled

33

steadily against the strong current. Presently he rested on his oars and drifted a minute.

"Look," he said, "where the bank is steep—there is mother and baby."

"Which side?" began Philippa eagerly, and then she saw them, a swan and her tiny cygnet swimming slowly past.

Simon leaned forward and wished with all his heart that he had a camera. That picture would have been something very special.

"There are more babies on the river. Little ducks. Perhaps we see some," Peter told them, and Simon began to feel excited. If he could persuade Hans Uli to come down here, they might get the photograph he wanted just by sitting on the bank.

A moment later they were shouting to make an echo as they slipped under the bridge. They were scarcely out on the other side when Simon cried, "Look! Look—there's the little green carriage! Mr. Berg is going over the river. Hi! Mr. Berg."

"He doesn't see down here," said Philippa, "he's too busy driving Eiger."

"Mr. Berg's carriage but not Mr. Berg I think," Peter told them, "he is gone to visit his married daughter in Italy, so his brother, Old Dani, looks after the horses."

"Italy!" Simon sounded envious. "That's somewhere I want to see," he said fervently, remembering what he had heard Uncle Max say about it.

"You will—if you want it hard enough." Peter began to turn the boat and soon they were going easily with the fast flowing water.

"I must go back to work," he told them, "and I think that for you Hans Uli will come. Have you liked the river?"

"It's gorgeous, thank you," they both told him with delight.

The church clock struck four, and Simon was getting very restless before Hans Uli appeared in the little yard.

His camera was slung over his shoulder in its neat brown case, and he was puffing because he had run all the way.

"Where's Kati?" asked Philippa promptly, and Hans Uli made a gesture of despair.

"Kati is because I am late," he declared, getting his English very mixed in his effort to explain. "She has fallen down all the steps and her head is . . . " he banged his own head with his fist as a substitute for the word he needed.

"Oh, poor Kati! Does she want me to go and play with her?" asked Philippa hopefully, but Hans Uli shook his head.

"She lies down," he said, "Helga says sleep is good."

"Then I'll come with you," announced Philippa, and the boys looked at each other in dismay.

"This is our secret," said Simon rebelliously, but Hans Uli was used to his sisters getting their own way. "It's no matter, let her come," he said.

He led them out of the yard, and was going in the opposite direction to the square, but Simon tugged his sleeve.

"Come this way! Down to the river!" he begged. "There's a swan down there with one tiny one, and Peter says there are ducklings—he took us for a row this morning. Surely a swan would be special?"

"A swan!" Hans Uli stopped and thought a moment. "A swan with a small one? That would be good if we were close."

To Simon's delight he agreed, and five minutes later they were walking along the river bank, straining their eyes for a glimpse of something white.

The tree shaded path beside the water was very quiet, and the scent of honeysuckle and lilac came from gardens which lay behind the hedge. The boys marched along, each anxious to be the first to see the swan, but Philippa lagged behind, looking for flowers in the grass, and feeling too hot to hurry.

"Wait a minute!" she called, "I've got grit in my shoe—you're going too fast."

"Oh, come on, we can't hang about," Simon called back crossly, and then, as she bent to unbuckle her sandal Philippa saw it—a beady black eye watching her from a clump of reeds.

Forgetting the piece of grit she raced after the boys.

"Come back!" she urged, "Come quietly, the swan is there—we've passed her."

On tiptoe they crept back. The beady eye had disappeared, but when Hans Uli trod cautiously to the edge of the bank a long neck appeared, and the swan hissed gently. Hastily he retreated.

"This way," he whispered and went a few yards further down. The bank curved very slightly and there was a boat moored to a stout post opposite a garden gate.

Very carefully Hans Uli crawled into it, and crouching down he took his camera from its case. Anxiously the other two watched him as he peered through his view finder.

"Can you see her?" breathed Simon.

"I see them both, but they are too far away," Hans Uli sounded glum. "If only we had some bread she would come near," he said sadly.

"I have some. I saved it from dinner in case we met Eiger," Philippa announced calmly, and dragged a piece from the small pocket in her shorts.

"Coo! You've got brains!" Even Simon sounded admiring as he reached out his hand for it.

"I can throw it further," he told her, but Philippa wouldn't give it up. Breaking off a tiny piece she tossed it towards the reeds. For a moment nothing happened, and then there was a movement and a ripple and the swan came silently towards them.

Hans Uli was so excited that he could hardly steady the camera as Philippa threw another piece nearer to the boat.

To her joy the small grey cygnet came close behind its mother, and she aimed her last piece hoping it would swim into the picture.

The swan's long neck was arched, and Hans Uli's finger trembled on the catch, when suddenly, on the other side of the path, a gate opened. Out came an old lady with a watering can in one hand, and a long handled scoop in the other.

"Wait! Wait!" cried Simon, but she only smiled, and said something in German. The next moment the long scoop smacked down into the water. With a great flapping of wings the swan showed its displeasure, and then, with its young one close behind it, it headed down the river.

Rocking the boat violently Hans Uli said something which sounded very angry, Simon stamped his foot in disgust, and Philippa tried not to burst into tears.

Apparently unaware of the trouble she had caused, the old lady scooped water into her can and went back across the lane, leaving three desolate children. The swan would not return.

"It's unfair," stormed Hans Uli. "Always I am unfortunate. If Johannes had been taking that picture the old woman would not have come—I know it!"

Simon was very sorry for him, and unhappy, because the swan had been his idea. Now perhaps Hans Uli would not want his company any more. It was a pity, he thought gloomily, that their friend believed so firmly that he was unfortunate. "I know Daddy would say that had nothing to do with it—it could have happened to anybody."

Although it was just as hot as ever the beautiful day seemed suddenly clouded, because they were all feeling cross.

The Green Mountain

5 FOR SOME MINUTES THEY STOOD FUMING.
"There might be ducks further up," suggested Simon, rather flatly, but Hans Uli wanted to get away from the river.

Suddenly his determined look came back again, he slung the camera-case round his neck and set off very quickly along the path.

"I know a better place," he said, "perhaps we see big butterflies, or a wild goat . . . "

He walked so fast that the others had to trot to keep up with him, and it was really too hot for that.

"Where are we going?" Philippa kept asking, but he would only say, "You shall see."

A few minutes later they left the river path and crossed a busy main road, which curved round, hugging the steep rocky side of the mountain. Hans Uli was very careful about that road even though he was in a hurry. He waited till a gang of roadmenders were going across and then said "Run now!" and pushed the other two in front of him.

"How much further do we have to walk?" demanded Philippa, who was wishing she had stayed with Grandmother.

"No further. We are there."

Hans Uli led them up some steps and paused near the top. "Have you money?" he asked.

"Money? No, Grandmother pays for everything—what do we want money for?"

The place looked like a tiny railway station. High above it, and closing it in on all sides, the great forest of firs and pines and larches clothed the mountain with thick, soft green.

"We go up by train because it is steep, but we walk down," Hans Uli explained, turning out his pockets in search of the last of his pocket-money. Simon was delighted. This was a dream come true, something he had wanted since he looked out of the window on that very first morning. But Philippa stood very still and tense, she was not happy at all.

Hans Uli was frowning over the coins in his hand, when Simon remembered that he was not quite penniless.

"I've got two francs!" he cried, "Uncle Max gave them to me on the plane—I'd forgotten."

They were still in the pocket of his green holiday shorts, and Hans Uli looked relieved. "Plenty for both as you are young," he said, and marched towards the ticket office.

"I don't want to go," said Philippa suddenly. "I'll sit here and wait for you—or I'll go back to Grandma—I shan't get lost, truly I shan't."

At that moment a good-natured looking man in a peaked cap beckoned to them to hurry. He seemed to know Hans Uli. "Don't be cuckoo!" said Simon with disgust, and as Hans Uli came running with the tickets he pushed Philippa in front of him towards the waiting carriages.

It was a very strange train. The hillside was so steep that the little red coaches with white roofs were built so that they were one above the other. The journey was very steady and slow, with the great trunks of the trees crowding close on either side, but every now and then they caught a glimpse of the little town, and the river far, far below.

"It's wizard!" said Simon, flattening his nose against the window in an effort to see the church clock down there, and perhaps even the hotel where Grandmother was.

Suddenly he turned his attention to Philippa.

"You look like you're going to be sick," he said bluntly.

Philippa bit her lip. "I don't think I like being up so high, and—it's—it's so thick . . . "

"It is good after the first time," Hans Uli assured her, "I come many times—here is the top."

All the holiday-makers on the train went streaming away towards a bright little cafe set among the trees, but Hans Uli had no time for coffee and cream cakes.

"We find the path and do not talk," he said, and led them along a narrow little track thick with pine needles and fallen cones. For a short way it was level, and twisted in and out among the thickets taking them away from the sounds of laughter into deeper and deeper stillness.

Rays of sunlight touched young larches and brightened their new green till they were almost golden, and the drowsy hum of insects was soon the only sound.

And then Philippa saw violets. Little drifts of them grew close to great knotted tree roots, and beside mossy boulders, such big wild violets that she called the boys to look.

For Hans Uli they were just a part of every spring, but Simon was astonished. "I'm sure we don't have violets in the pinewood near home," he said, and even helped to pick a few for Phillipa who was gathering them as fast as she could.

"For Grandma—for her little pink vase," she said, and for the moment she forgot her fear of the forest.

"Now we are quiet!" Hans Uli urged again, and they turned on to a track that went so steeply down that Philippa couldn't suppress a little squeak.

Suddenly feeling sorry for her, in spite of his impatience, Simon reached out a hand. "Hang on to my shirt at the back," he whispered, "then you can't fall."

Slowly and quietly they followed Hans Uli. In spite of his tough boots he walked very lightly. Suddenly there was a slight scuttering sound ahead, and without needing to be warned they all stood quite still.

Up the trunk of a young larch, very close to them, sped a squirrel, and stopped a moment on a low branch to stare at them with its bright eyes. Simon had a job not to exclaim aloud, for the little creature was jet black.

Cautiously Hans Uli raised his camera, but even as he

steadied it the squirrel was gone. One leap took it to the next tree, and it was lost among the green.

"This is my bad day," said Hans Uli despondently, "the special things are there, but not for me."

It seemed as if he was right, for a robin came to sing on a boulder showing his red breast so clearly, but he was too far away. A great black and yellow butterfly flitted round them, but refused to settle anywhere.

Holding tight to Simon's green check shirt Philippa was less fearful, they went so slowly, and Hans Uli seemed so sure of himself. Presently they found a wider path again, and followed as it turned upwards, leading them higher and higher.

Suddenly Simon stopped, and forgot to be silent. There was an opening in the trees, and down below stretched a magnificent view. A wide blue lake with a toy-sized steamer moving across it, and beyond the mountain ranges which were mirrored in the water.

"Oh wait! Wait Hans Uli!" he cried. "It's nearly too lovely to be true."

"You are tourists," said Hans Uli, sounding superior. "I do not notice it all the time. If you shout like that you will drive away things for my picture."

Simon flushed, but Philippa was not listening to the rebuke, she had found something that interested her. A little seat had been built into a rock outcrop, and above it, cut in the rock, was a long band of lettering in old-fashioned German script.

"What's that? What does it say?" she demanded, tracing the letters with her finger.

"That. Oh, it is nothing," said Hans Uli crossly, "you can stay here if you wish and look at your view, but I must work for my picture."

"You're grumpy," Simon told him bluntly. "We're coming too, but you might tell us what this says first. I can see 'Gott' and I know that means God, it's like your balcony."

Hans Uli translated with a bad grace. "It says 'Stand here and see the wonderful works of God'. Now will you hurry!"

"It's nice," said Philippa, satisfied. "God made the mountains, and the little ants, and the violets, it's a nice place for people to sit and say 'thank You'. I wish He hadn't made this mountain quite so steep though," she added anxiously, as the path took a sudden dip. "Let me hold your shirt again Simon—it helps me not to feel sick."

And then it happened. From somewhere high above them came a sharp crack, the snapping of a big branch, and Philippa screamed. Before the boys could stop her she turned and began to run.

Back along the track she went, plunging downwards and losing the path. Then she lost her footing as well on the slippery pine needles and went rolling down a terrifying slope.

It was a fallen pine tree which stopped her. It lay across her path with bracken growing thickly beside its rotting trunk. Philippa subsided into it like a green cushion, and sat up trembling. She was scratched and bruised, but not badly hurt, though she was sobbing with terror.

Slipping and sliding the boys went after her, Simon with his heart thumping, and Hans Uli saying angry things in German all the way down. "You little silly! What made you do that?" shouted Simon, as he slid the last few yards to join her, and then he realised what she was saying through chattering teeth.

"Bears!" she was sobbing. "Bears! Oh! Hans Uli, will they kill us?"

"Bears!" exclaimed Hans Uli, arriving with a thud beside her, "there are no bears here."

Simon looked very scornful. "Bears you little silly—did you think that noise we heard was bears coming after us? Of course it wasn't—there aren't any here."

"There *are* bears," gulped Philippa, struggling to her feet. "When we saw all the ones in the carving shop I asked

Grandma where they lived, and she said 'in the high forest', and this is the high forest. Hans Uli I want to go home."

For answer Hans Uli sat down among the bracken and pulled her down beside him, just as though she were Kati. "Long ago bears were here, but not now," he said kindly, and quite firmly. "Bears are everywhere in my country, but they are wooden ones."

Philippa looked very hard into his steady grey eyes. She wanted to be quite sure that he was speaking the truth, for ever since they first boarded the little train the thought of bears had been in her mind. She knew quite well that God made the bears as well as the violets, but she couldn't help being afraid of them. After all, forests belonged to bears, and the towns belonged to people.

"There is nothing," Hans Uli assured her, "I know it, because my father would have told me. Also we had to write a paper—a lesson? How do you say it?"

"An essay?" suggested Simon, busy breaking pieces of rotten bark from the massive trunk he was sitting on.

"An essay? That is a strange name. Well we must write one last winter about animals in our canton—I got good marks. I made a long list, but no bears."

"How did you know?" persisted Philippa. "There might be some on the other mountains. Did you find all about them in a lesson book?"

"Not me!" shrugged Hans Uli. "Johannes did, he reads all the books, he is like an old man, making many notes. I have seen them when he was not looking, and he has written 'no bears' and 'none seen for very many years' so I did not put them in, and I got good marks."

"But that was cheating!" cried Simon, horrified. "You got good marks for work you didn't do yourself."

"Reading many books is too hard," muttered Hans Uli, beginning to frown again. "Johannes is clever, he reads all day, but he cannot make whistles like I can," he added defensively.

43

Philippa began pulling the pine needles out of her hair, and she looked at him very thoughtfully while she did so.

"I guess I know why you don't want to think about God," she said at last. "You know that cheating and lying and being lazy isn't the sort of thing that Jesus wants us to do. Cheating is another way of telling a lie Uncle Max says . . . "

"Don't preach, Philippa," Simon told her, not wishing to make Hans Uli angry again, but Philippa, who had stopped being frightened, was worried about their new friend.

"I'm not preaching," she said anxiously, "only I know I'm not happy when I do things that I'm sure aren't right—and besides, God gives us such a lot of lovely things—it seems mean not to love Him and do what He wants . . . "

"You speak too fast for me," mumbled Hans Uli, who had heard perfectly well, "I'm not sitting here any longer. If you want to get off the mountain you had better follow me."

He sounded gruff, but he helped Philippa to her feet before he turned to go. "You will not run again," he said. "You will walk as I do, carefully."

Philippa nodded. "I'm not afraid any more," she told him, "only of falling."

"You won't fall if you don't go dashing around," teased Simon. "What did you expect to see? A bear about as big as Mr. Berg's old Eiger?"

Hans Uli, going ahead, stopped in his tracks. "You know Mr. Berg?" he said, surprised.

"Grandma took us for a ride, and he fetched us in the little green carriage," explained Simon.

"I like Eiger . . . " began Hans Uli, and then suddenly he shouted, "That's it! I have found the 'special'. Mr. Berg has it—because of you I am reminded."

"What is it?" asked Simon eagerly, and even Philippa was surprised out of listening for sudden sounds.

"It is a carving," Hans Uli explained, "it is so old that it has belonged to Mr. Berg's family many grandfathers back.

It is a little market with houses round—it even has a fountain. He has shown it to me many times when I was small. He blows much dust off it every time because he keeps it in the stable. It is on a high shelf, and he forgets it."

"But would it make your special picture?" Philippa looked puzzled, but Hans Uli explained eagerly, "I shall dust and polish it, and then set it in the sun and take it close . . . "

He pretended to hold a camera a couple of feet from Philippa's face. "I have a thing for close pictures," he told them proudly, "it makes them good. It will look a real town, only it is of wood. Nobody will have one like it."

"Will Mr. Berg let you have it? Can I see it when he does?"

Simon hoped that he might be allowed to go to the stable and help borrow it. Hans Uli was quite sure there would be no difficulty. "We are friends," he said, "often I brush Eiger and Berne, and I dust the green carriage. He will let me have it—we will go now and ask."

"But Mr. Berg isn't there," said Philippa, "Peter told us today. He's gone to see his daughter in Italy, someone else is driving Eiger."

The happy look left Hans Uli's face. "That will be Old Dani," he muttered gloomily. "Old Dani and I are NOT friends—he does not like boys."

"But Mr. Berg will be back again in a little while won't he?" Simon said.

"It is too long till he comes back, always he goes for three weeks. It is too long, there must be time for the picture to be—to be—" Hans Uli looked even more gloomy because he couldn't find the right word.

"Developed," prompted Simon, holding Philippa steady while she emptied pine needles out of her shoes.

There was nothing more to say. Their hunt for something special, and all their bright ideas, had come to nothing. In single file they scrambled down the narrow track until they could hear the traffic on the road below. They were silent because they were disappointed, and even the sunshine didn't seem so bright.

Simon was the least sad of the three, because now, when he saw the green mountain from his bedroom window he would know what it was like up there. He would think of the little black squirrel, and remember the huge mossy boulders which stood among the trees.

Then Hans Uli stopped and looked back, and he was smiling again.

"It will be all right," he said cheerfully. "My father will ask Old Dani for the carving, I am sure of it. He comes home tomorrow night, and Old Dani would lend it to him. He knows that my father is Mr. Berg's good friend, so I shall have my picture."

It seemed a long way home, and Philippa began to limp, because she had twisted her foot in falling. She felt sure that Grandmother would not be pleased to see the state that her clothes and socks were in, and said so to Simon as they trailed wearily along beside the river.

But Simon refused to be gloomy. "Grandma climbed too," he reminded her, "and I guess she didn't keep clean all the time."

Hans Uli said goodbye to them when they reached the cobbled square, and as he went away they could hear him whistling.

"I wish he didn't cheat," said Simon, frowning, as they watched him go, "one day he's bound to be found out, and then Helga will be awfully upset. I like Helga."

Philippa didn't answer, but as she limped on over the cobbles she thought about it. "I know what my special prayer is going to be tonight," she said, "we always have 'specials' at home. Tonight mine is going to be for Hans Uli."

"That he finds a good picture?" asked Simon.

"No," said Philippa, "that he finds Jesus."

Behind the Woodpile

6 A DISAPPOINTMENT WAS IN STORE FOR the children next day. They had planned to watch for the swan, but Grandmother had arranged for them to go visiting.

"I want some old friends of mine to see you both while you're here," she said. "They knew your father, Simon, when he was small, and Philippa's mother too, and they asked me to bring you."

"Will it take long?" asked Simon gloomily, and Philippa wanted to know "How far?"

"Not very far, but they will send a car to fetch us, and for once I want you to behave nicely ALL the time."

So there was no getting out of it. Grandmother's friends were kind, but they were elderly, and their house was 'just an ordinary house' Philippa complained in a whisper.

By that she meant that it was a modern bungalow with a lovely garden, but no exciting balconies, and not even a woodpile.

Both children were glad when lunch and tea were over, and the car arrived to take them home.

"Hans Uli may have been and gone away again, we're so late," fretted Simon, but when they reached the hotel no one had seen anything of Hans Uli at all.

"There is some trouble for Klaus Werner I think," said Peter, looking unusually serious, "something I have heard on the radio about Professor Stahel. Perhaps Hans Uli must stay at home tonight, Helga may want him."

But Hans Uli did arrive, ten minutes later, looking very troubled. As soon as she saw him Philippa gave a cry of delight, for he was wearing a velvet jacket with scarlet braid.

"Oh that's pretty!" she exclaimed, and Simon, though secretly admiring it, asked bluntly, "What have you got that on for?"

"Because this afternoon I sing with the Young Folk Singers, and I am not yet home. I am late, and there is trouble also. My father will not be back tonight."

"Peter said there was trouble, but he didn't tell us what. Is he ill?" asked Simon, while Philippa gazed at the jacket with its short puff sleeves, brass buttons, and alpine flowers beautifully embroidered on the lapels. Hans Uli's spotless white shirt sleeves came down below those strange short ones, and his ordinary breeches, socks, and heavy boots made a workaday contrast.

"Does everyone wear a jacket like this to sing in?" she wanted to know, more interested in the jacket than in Klaus Werner's trouble.

"All the boys. But this was mine before I began singing with the folk group. My uncle has given it to me because I have been to the mountains. Last spring I helped with the cattle, and it was for 'thank you'. It gets tight now," he added, wriggling his shoulders, "but that is no matter—it is trouble for Professor Stahel that matters. Also because my father is not home he cannot ask Old Dani for the carving, and for me that is bad."

"What's happened? Can we come with you just the same?" asked Simon, anxiously, and was relieved when Hans Uli answered quickly, "I want you, I want you to help me. My sisters are no good. You will come home while I take this off?"

He gave his jacket a proud pat, and Philippa whisked away to tell Grandmother that they would be at the chalet with Helga and Kati.

"And that's a good thing," said Grandmother, looking up from the pullover she was knitting for Simon, "I hear from Peter that there is some trouble at Professor Stahel's chalet.

If Mr. Werner cannot get home, Helga may be glad for you to cheer them up."

When Philippa rejoined the boys they all set off as fast as they could.

"I take you a quick way," Hans Uli told them, and trotted through some narrow, twisty alleyways, dodged across somebody's yard, and came out beside a long building which had a carved horse's head over its doorway. Rows of stalls could be dimly seen inside.

"This must be where Berne and Eiger live," guessed Philippa, but she was wrong. "This is the big stables, it belongs to another man," Hans Uli told them. "Many horses and carriages here, but Mr. Berg has a little stable, I will show you soon."

He ran up a narrow pathway between the two high fences, and then to their surprise he opened a little gate behind the apple tree in his own yard. The hay was piled in little haycocks, smelling wonderful in the sun, and the tortoiseshell cat blinked down at them from the balcony.

"Wait, while I speak to Helga," commanded Hans Uli, and ran up the wooden stairway. They could hear Kati singing, which sounded as though her head was better, and not at all as though her father was ill.

"What is the matter with him?" Philippa asked Simon, certain that Hans Uli must have explained.

"It's not anything wrong with Mr. Werner, it's something that's disappeared from Professor Stahel's chalet in the mountains—something he's been working on for ages Hans Uli says. I don't really understand, but I think it's papers that have been lost. I guess he writes down all the things he invents.

"Like recipes when Mummy cooks?" suggested Philippa.

"Something like that. Very precious and very secret Hans Uli says they are, and someone must have wanted them. He says the chalet is all over policemen, and Mr. Werner can't come back because he might have to drive the Professor to the airport, or somewhere. At least he thinks that's why."

"Hullo!" called Kati from above at that moment. "You come to play?"

Philippa ran up to her, eager to look at the cuckoo clock again, but Simon sat down on the lowest step and waited. He liked it there in the sun, and the cat came down to join him.

"This is nicer than the whole day has been," he was thinking, and then he heard Hans Uli clattering along the balcony. The velvet jacket had been changed for an ordinary shirt, and Hans Uli was devouring a hunk of bread and cheese. He was looking both troubled and angry.

"Some for you," he said, offering Simon a split roll, and then he sat down on the step and ate for a moment in silence.

"It is bad about my father," he said at last. "Kati is too young, she is not told, but Helga tells me because I am the boy. My father cannot come home because the policemen think he might have taken those precious papers—my FATHER! Are they mad? He would not take anything that was not his—not even a tiny thing—he would never tell a lie or cheat anybody, he is a Werner!"

Simon looked at Hans Uli as he sat there with a proud, angry look on his face, and he couldn't help thinking of the essay, and the bears.

It seemed as though Hans Uli read his thoughts, for suddenly he flushed to the roots of his hair. "You are a Werner too," said Simon in a small voice, and Hans Uli turned away, and put his hands over his face.

When he took them away again the flush had gone, and he was very white.

"I'll never cheat again, never," he said violently, "I know my father is good, so I must be, even if it is hard. If God will let those papers be found, then I will work so well . . . "

"I guess that working hard anyway would be best," suggested Simon.

Hans Uli didn't answer at once. He sat kicking stones with the toe of his heavy boot. "It is possible you are right," he said at last, and stood up. "For now," he announced, "I am going to work on my picture. If it is good it will be something to make my father glad. You will help me?"

"I said I would, but what am I helping you with? Is Philippa coming too?"

"No, No! Not girls!" Hand Uli beckoned him to come and sit under the apple tree. "I am getting the carving from Mr. Berg without telling Old Dani," he explained. "It is not necessary, and he cannot say 'no' if he is not asked. I only borrow it because I know that Mr. Berg will say 'yes'. Together we will go to the stable and you will help me reach it. Perhaps after I have taken my picture I put it back. Perhaps I wait till Mr. Berg comes home . . . "

Hans Uli paused, considering, and Simon said anxiously, "But that's a kind of stealing, isn't it? Do you think we ought to? And won't Old Dani see it isn't there? Surely it's wrong to take a thing without asking?"

"Stealing is wrong, but it is not stealing if one gives back. It is not wrong because I know Mr. Berg is glad about it. If the picture is fine he will be very happy. We must hurry because it is easy for us now. Helga has just told me that Old Dani has gone by with Berne—he will be a long while, because he has gone to—to the . . . "

He lifted up his foot, and pretended to hammer the sole of his shoe.

"To the blacksmith's for new shoes," said Simon. "So there's just Eiger in the stable?"

"Just Eiger. I like him best. He is more gentle when I brush him. Let us go."

He opened the gate, and as they went through they heard Philippa calling. "We can see you," she shouted. "Can we come too?"

"You are not wanted," Hans Uli told her rudely, and the

boys began to run. Simon was still uneasy, but as Hans Uli seemed so sure that Mr. Berg would be pleased, he supposed it was all right.

Mr. Berg's small stable was tucked away under the shade of a great tree, with a long stone water trough against one of its old walls. The little green carriage stood in the yard in front of it, with some old wheels and shafts, a small barrow, and a very neat manure heap. The half door was closed and bolted, and the boys could hear Eiger stamping a little in his stall, as he munched his hay.

"We will get in from the back," said Hans Uli, "that bolt is stiff and I am not so high that I can lean over and pull it. Besides, Madam Knoble across the road could see us. She sits on her balcony and sees everything."

He led the way down a narrow passage which smelt strongly of hay and horses, and there, under a sloping roof, was the great woodpile which every Swiss has for winter fuel. The logs were neatly stacked, but they did not reach to the roof, and Hans Uli began scrambling up to work himself into the space between.

"You come," he called down, "it is easy—up here no one sees us . . . "

Very puzzled, Simon followed him, and soon saw the reason for the climb. High up in the stable wall was a window space. It had no glass in it, but Hans Uli explained that in the winter a great wooden shutter was fixed there, and in summer the horses liked the air.

"I can get through," he said, "my feet find the top of Berne's stall—then I jump. You come—it is easy . . . "

Simon wasn't so sure. It didn't seem easy at all, but Hans Uli disappeared so quickly that he crawled forward and looked down.

The stable was dim, but plenty of light for their purpose came from the half door, through which he could see the yard. The old stout timbers of the stall were just below him, and Hans Uli was looking up ready to guide his feet. He heard Eiger give a faint whinny and saw his black head toss above the middle partition.

"Hurry!" urged Hans Uli, and rolling over, Simon clutched the nearest log and pushed his feet through the hole. A moment later he landed softly in the straw. His heart was thumping, but it began to seem a good adventure.

Hans Uli had crossed over to the other side of the building where hay rakes and harness hung from pegs. Above, quite close to the tiles of the roof ran a wide shelf. Simon could see boxes and bottles, and dusty mysterious packages up there, and at one end something large and wooden.

"That's it—it is the back—the carving is to the wall," Hans Uli told him. "Old Dani will never look up there, those are forgotten things. Now you must help me, it is heavy."

Pulling an old wheelbarrow from the corner Hans Uli found a small crate to put across it, and with Simon steadying him he climbed cautiously up to stand on the box.

He reached up, just able to touch the smooth dark wood of Mr. Berg's ancient treasure. "I am too low still," he grunted, and got down again.

Searching round he found a box of dandy brushes, and that he thought would give him a few more inches. Up he climbed, with anxious help from Simon, and wobbled a little as he straightened.

This time he could lean against the shelf, and as he pulled the heavy old carving towards him dust rose in clouds.

"Atishoo! Atishoo!" Hans Uli sneezed violently, and at that moment the sound of hoofs clattering came from the yard outside.

Simon heard a deep voice talking to a horse.

"Old Dani! He's back!" gasped Hans Uli between the sneezes, and tried to get down quickly.

In his haste he pulled the great block of wood that was balanced just above him, and his cry of terror as it tipped rang through the stable.

With a great crash the shelf came down, and Hans Uli with it. Simon jumped aside as the carving hit the floor, and Eiger plunged with fright in his stall, his great hoofs drumming on the manger.

With a shout Old Dani drew the bolt and rushed in. Hans Uli sprawled senseless on the cobblestones with Simon trembling beside him.

Mr. Berg's treasure was split in three pieces.

Surprise for Simon

7 IT WAS AT THAT MOMENT THAT PHILIPPA appeared, with Kati very white and frightened at her heels.

"Is Hans Uli dead?" she gasped, as Old Dani carefully rolled him over, and Kati hid her eyes in her scarlet apron and burst into tears.

Old Dani was saying violent things in a deep growly voice, though Simon couldn't understand a word. But Kati could. Her sobs suddenly ceased and she became angry instead.

"Nein! Nein!" she cried, stamping her foot, and caught Simon's sleeve, tugging it and demanding, "Tell him Hans Uli never steal!"

But it was Philippa who faced the furious old man.

"Hans Uli and Simon were borrowing," she told him, "borrowing! Do you understand? Mr. Berg would lend things, but they knew you wouldn't, so they borrowed to put back—I know all about it—it was just because you're horrible and mean and . . . "

She paused for breath, a little shocked at her own boldness.

Fortunately Old Dani understood very little of what she said, but he realised that Simon was asking urgently, "Is he dead? He isn't dead, is he?"

"No—I do not think . . . " he grunted, getting stiffly to his feet. "Go to Helga—the telephone . . . "

"The doctor," said Simon, but Kati had vanished before he could start, and Philippa raced after her.

Sadly Simon gathered up the broken carving, trying to fit the heavy pieces together, glancing from Hans Uli's still, white face to Old Dani's red angry one.

"Give me that," commanded the old man, taking the pieces from him, and Simon felt sick and miserable. What Grandmother would say he just couldn't imagine.

But it was quite a long time before he saw Grandmother to tell her about it. Helga came panting into the stable in a very few minutes, and the doctor and an ambulance were not far behind. People began to gather in the yard, curious to know what had happened.

Poor Helga, chalky white with anxiety, saw her brother gently placed on a stretcher, and wondered how she was going to tell her father. Already there was trouble enough for Klaus Werner.

She got into the ambulance and was driven away.

"Stay with Kati for a little while till I get back," she had begged Simon, and to Simon's relief she had assured Old Dani that the boys had no intention of stealing. Philippa had made her understand as they hurried to the stable, and Simon was thankful that she had been with them when Hans Uli first thought of the carving.

"But how did you know that we were in the stable just now?" he asked her, as the three trailed sadly back towards the chalet.

Philippa looked mischievous.

"When Hans Uli was rude and said he didn't want us, we stalked you. We saw you get up the woodpile, but you didn't see us—we were too clever. Then Kati saw Berne coming back and we ran and hid in Madame Knoble's passage, but when we heard the crash, and Old Dani shouting, Kati wouldn't keep still. She said Hans Uli was being hurt, and she was going to save him."

"And I thought girls were just soppy . . . " muttered Simon.

They waited about on the balcony, watching the street and feeling miserable, too miserable to invent a game. The cuckoo clock struck five and six, and even seven, but still Helga had not come.

Kati and Philippa had tried to cheer things up by getting a meal. Kati had put out bread, butter and cheese, and some cold sausage. Philippa poured out three mugs of milk, without slopping any on the table, and loaded up a tray.

She carried it out on to the balcony, and the tortoise-shell cat followed, mewing.

"It's hungry," she said, "poor pussy—can I give her some Kati?"

So Kati found a dish and they poured out more milk, and chopped small pieces of sausage. The cat sniffed them, and turned away with an expression of disgust.

"I guess it has pepper in it," said Simon. "Grandma says they're different from English sausages—maybe she eats cheese."

The little cat did eat cheese, and for a while they were almost happy taking turns to feed her.

"The rabbits! They hunger too," said Kati suddenly, remembering that Hans Uli should have fed them long ago. So they all went down the steps and round to the hutches where the rabbits were certainly looking very anxious. Kati rummaged round among some wooden boxes and found a store of cabbage leaves and crusts, which Helga had put ready.

Simon liked undoing the hutches and putting some green-stuff in each one, watching the twitching noses of the rabbits as they started to nibble.

But Philippa didn't help. She had a nasty cold, unhappy, feeling about Hans Uli, and what his father would say when he came home. "Oh, God, please don't let him be badly hurt—let him be able to be mended," she prayed silently. "Please let him be able to play again and feed his rabbits—and please let him think about Jesus, and know that He loves him . . . "

"Kati? Simon? Are you there?" said a voice which startled them, and made Simon shut the hutch door in a hurry. Round the corner of the house came Peter. He had been sent from the hotel because Grandmother was getting worried.

He looked very troubled indeed when things were explained to him by all three at once, in two different languages.

"A bad ending to a not so good idea," he said, "and very bad trouble for Helga just now I think . . . "

As though she had heard her name, Helga came in at the garden gate.

"Oh, Helga! is he all right?" called Simon, and Kati went flying to meet her.

Helga still looked very white, but not quite so strained. "He is a little awake now," she told them, to Simon's great relief, "but his back is hurt. There must be X-rays, and it will be bed for Hans Uli for many days I think."

"Your father?" asked Peter, and Helga's chin quivered a little as she answered, "He is told. I have spoken on the 'phone, but he cannot come as Hans Uli is not in danger. All the people who were in Professor Stahel's chalet this morning must stay there I think—the police are asking so many questions. Tomorrow perhaps he will come home."

Simon thought that Helga did not look angry when she explained about her father, as Hans Uli had done, only very sad. "But she must know that he hasn't done anything wrong," he thought, "I would be sure my Daddy hadn't."

When the reached the hotel Grandmother was waiting under the trees leaning on her sticks. She had a scolding on the tip of her tongue, but when she saw how serious the three of them were she pointed to the little red chairs. "Sit down and tell me about if before you go to wash. You, too, Peter, if you can spare a minute."

So they told her, right from the beginning, and how necessary it had been for Hans Uli to find something special to photograph.

"And now it's broken to pieces," ended Simon sadly, "but we weren't stealing it Grandma, truly we weren't!"

"I'm quite sure of that, but borrowing without asking is always foolish—so many things can go wrong, and this time they went wrong indeed. Poor Hans Uli, one clever photograph wouldn't make up for some really hard work at his lessons, but I'm very sorry for him. This is a bad time for all of them I'm afraid."

Grandmother got up stiffly, and thanked Peter for his help.

"If there is any assistance you think I could give them, Peter . . ."

Simon heard the conversation, as they walked towards the door, "You don't think their father is really under any suspicion, do you?"

"I cannot tell," said Peter sadly, "but I know this—anyone who thinks Klaus Werner does wrong makes a big mistake."

Simon and Philippa generally had a game of some sort with Grandmother before bed. She had all sorts of games and quiz cards, dominoes, and spillikins tucked away in her bureau drawer, but that evening Simon couldn't settle to any of them. He left Philippa to have her hair washed, and wandered out by himself.

"Only as far as the square, to look at the fountain," he promised, and went slowly out into the scented dusk. It was cool after the heat of the day, and people sat on their balconies resting.

Simon, hands in pockets, kicked at the cobblestones moodily, almost wishing that the church clock would strike nine so that it was time for bed. He came near the corner where he had first met Hans Uli. "If I hadn't been staring up at the mountains he wouldn't have bumped into me," he thought, and glanced up to look at the great peaks once more.

He had the surprise of his life. They were not white any longer, but a wonderful, breathtaking pink. Down below in the valley, where he stood, the hills looked almost black, because the sun no longer shone on them, but up on those tremendous heights the sunset light lingered, turning the snow to fire. "It's—beautiful!" said Simon aloud, not quite sure what had caused the miracle. And then he realised that somebody was beside him, watching, too. Peter was going off duty for a little while.

"It comes every night when it is fine," Peter told him, "and it tells us that tomorrow will be fine too. Perhaps it will be a happier day for you, with good news of Hans Uli. I can tell you one thing," he added, and paused, with his well-known smile creasing his jolly face.

"What thing? Tell me?" urged Simon eagerly.

"A good thing," said Peter with conviction, "you will come back to Switzerland—if anyone sees the alpine glow on the mountains, then they must come back."

When Simon woke next morning he lay a moment looking across at the green hill, and then slipped out of bed and went to the window. It was another gloriously sunny morning, and Hans Uli would have to spend it in hospital.

He wondered what Mr. Berg would say when he heard about all that had happened yesterday, and he wondered if the beautiful carving could ever be mended. Thinking of the carving made him remember the shop with the bears, Grandmother had promised to buy him a bear of some sort before he went home. Perhaps he could persuade her to take them there today, and to have more cream cakes at the cafe with the striped umbrellas.

But even that idea didn't make him feel entirely happy, so instead he tried to think what kind of present he could buy for Hans Uli which would really cheer him up.

"Coo - - - ee!" called a voice from below, and there was Philippa, dressed already, and urging him to hurry.

"Grandma says she has a special treat for us, because she thinks we're feeling a bit dismal after yesterday," she shouted. "She says put on your clean shorts and your socks to match."

"Why? Where are we going?" demanded Simon, nearly falling out of the window. But Philippa didn't know, and she raced round the corner to be first in the dining-room for breakfast.

Stormy Weather

8

"I HAVE PLENTY OF TIME FREE TO entertain you today," Grandmother told them, and the sun shone in on to the breakfast table promising the very best kind of day for any adventure.

"Where are we going?" they kept begging her to tell them, but it was not until they were in the taxi that Simon found out. It was an ordinary taxi this time, not the little green carriage, and although Philippa was disappointed, Simon was very glad not to have to meet Old Dani again so soon.

As they drove away, the taximan, who also knew Grandmother very well, said cheerfully, "The sailings are very popular this season, Madame."

Sailings! Simon remembered the folders in the hall at the hotel which advertised trips on the twin lakes. "We're going on the water," he shouted. "We are, aren't we, Grandma? On a big boat, not just one like Peter's?"

"Too bad! I thought I really had kept a secret this time. Yes, we're going on a lake steamer, sailing most of the day, but we'll land at one of the villages and have a picnic by the shore. I thought it would be a pity to miss such a perfect day when it's as calm as a mill-pond. The reflection of the hills is always wonderful in weather like this."

They tumbled out of the taxi when it drew up beside a ticket office, and raced across to the water's edge while Grandmother paid the driver.

The big white pleasure steamer with its gay awnings was already filling with people, and Philippa was enchanted at the idea of going on board. "It looks smashing," agreed Simon, "but the water looks frightfully tame—it's so narrow—the people in the houses on the other side could swim across to here."

But he soon cheered up. "This is only the canal," Grandmother told them, as she hobbled across from the ticket office, "soon we will be out in the lake, and we'll be on it most of the day."

They hastened up the gangway, and ran around trying all the seats until Grandmother stopped them. "Sit here and behave," she told Simon, grabbing him as he ran by. So they subsided on to padded benches on either side of a narrow table, and found that they could kneel and look over the side quite comfortably.

It was intensely hot. Even the table was hot to the touch, and the sun was so bright that the water seemed to shimmer.

"It will be better when we start, just moving will make a breeze."

"When we get started there is a little counter through in the saloon where you can buy lemonade . . . " began Grandmother, when something else happened which made them forget that they were thirsty. A crowd of children began coming on board, clattering up the gangway, chattering and laughing, the boys pushing each other to get the best places. They all wore heavy-nailed boots, even the little girls in their bright summer dresses, and each carried a satchel. The teachers, looking remarkably serene and cheerful in spite of the heat and the hubbub, shepherded them along towards the stern.

"They're going for a picnic, too. Will they get off where we do?"

Simon was wishing that he could join the boys, who looked all ready to go climbing. Four of the older ones wore velvet jackets like Hans Uli's and they had the heaviest boots of all.

"I expect they have helped with the cattle too . . . " Philippa suddenly jumped up and stood on her seat, "There's Kati!" she cried as the engines began to throb and they

63

slipped gently away from the quay, "there's Kati among the little ones!"

Kati heard her name and looked round, her small face flushing with pleasure. Her teacher looked round too, and Grandmother waved.

"That's Marie Knoble," she said, "I know her well, perhaps she will let Kati come and join us for a while." So Kati came, but she was shy. The other children turned and stared at her, and one or two giggled. After a few minutes she said good-bye and went back to her classmates. Kati at school and Kati at home must be two different people Philippa decided, so she turned her back on the party to look at the scenery.

Simon had no cause for disappointment now. They had passed out of the narrow canal into a vast blue lake, reflecting the bright sky. Far in the distance they could see the other shore, ringed with green hills. As they left the last few red roofed houses behind there was no beach or landing place, the steep slopes clothed with fir trees came down right to the water's edge.

"It's gorgeous!" murmured Simon, and even Philippa had quite forgotten about the lemonade. "Look," said Grandmother, "turn the other way. We are going to pass some foresters—look—they're making a raft."

She grabbed Simon's shirt and Phillipa's skirt as they both leaned out far over the rail in their eagerness to see.

Down the mountainside was a great brown scar of fallen tree trunks lying at all angles where they had been felled. Some had already rolled down into the water, and two men in a boat were pushing them about with poles. "They'll probably be floated all down the lake to a saw-mill," Grandmother told them, "it must be a very hard way of making a living."

"But fun," said Simon enviously, and thought how much Hans Uli would have enjoyed it. That threw a shadow over his happiness. Would his friend ever scramble about on steep places again, he wondered, or would he hobble with a stick, or even be in a wheelchair?

It was too bad to think about, so he went to join Philippa on the opposite side of the boat, wondering if Kati was thinking about Hans Uli too.

But at that moment Kati had something else to think about. A tall elderly man with a bright blue shirt, a rucksack, and a walking stick, had been talking to the teachers. Now he beckoned to the children to gather round him. "I wish he wasn't speaking German," whispered Philippa, "perhaps he's going to tell them a story . . . "

But it was not a story the other passengers heard. A folk song echoed joyfully across the deck, and another, and another, as the grey-haired man conducted his choir of eager children. Such gay, crisp songs, sung in clear well-trained voices, they brought a storm of clapping from all parts of the steamer as each one died away over the calm water.

"Hans Uli belongs to a Folk Group," whispered Simon, "perhaps those boys do. I wonder if Grandmother knows the words."

He went across to her, and found her sitting listening with a look of contentment on her face. "They're singing about their country," she said, "about the magnificent mountains, and the chamois, and the snow in wintertime.

"The wonderful works of God," said Philippa who had joined them, and her Grandmother turned to her with a warm smile. "So you found the little seat when you climbed with Hans Uli the other day? I think, if you remember it, that it will help you to enjoy beautiful things all your life."

"We're stopping! Do we have to get off?" cried Simon, disappointed.

"Not yet," he was told, as the boat tied up at the tiny jetty. Some of the passengers did go ashore there, and hurried away to a cluster of chalets, among the trees. Philippa was so busy watching them that the steamer was on its way before she realised that the grey-haired man had left them.

He stood on the jetty waving, and the schoolchildren crowded the rails waving back. Suddenly they began to sing again as the strip of water grew wider between them, and they went on singing till they could hardly see the colour of that bright blue shirt, and the walking stick being waved in farewell.

"Quite the nicest concert I can remember," said Grandmother, as the last notes died away.

"I'll always remember it," thought Philippa, and she smiled across at Kati and felt happy again.

The school disembarked at the next jetty, and went trailing off up a steep track till they were out of sight in the woods. "Hans Uli would have been one of them if we hadn't got into that stable," thought Simon, and was quite glad when the landing-stage was out of sight.

"Our village next," said Grandmother, "Kati will be able to tell you what they all did when you see her tonight. You must run round and ask how her brother is when we get back, and I expect Kati will be glad to have you to play with by then."

"We'll help her feed the rabbits," Simon decided, "and I guess that hay ought to be turned again." It was nice to know that there would be something to do after a lovely day, not just the hotel, the grown-up talk, and then bed.

It was quite a sizeable little pier that they saw ahead of them half an hour later. Chestnut trees edged the small quay, and there was even a motorbus waiting by some chalets at the water's edge. "I had to choose a place where there are seats," explained Grandmother, "the ground is too far down for me these days. I should never get up again."

She waited till the other passengers were off before she tackled the rather steep gangway, but Simon steadied her, and Philippa carried the picnic, and soon they were turning along the shore road under the trees. Every few yards there were low green seats, and there were hardly any people about because most of them had gone away on the motorbus.

Hungrily they spread their picnic, and then Philippa gave a cry of disgust. "I never bought my lemon on the boat! I forgot it, and now I'm starving thirsty. Why did you let me forget it, Grandma?"

"Silly child! You ought to be able to remember if you're thirsty or not." Grandmother sounded tetchy for once, but not for long. "There's a cafe just round the corner, and we'll all get something there. Then I want to take you to buy your presents from Switzerland from a real old woodcarver. I think you will like them better from a workshop than from the town."

"You're three times an angel," Simon told her, and jumped up to give her a squashing hug. He upset the basket and two tomatoes went bounding away into the water.

The woodcarver's workshop, when they found it a little later, was a dusty place full of the smell of sawdust and chippings. It seemed rather dim after the brightness outside, except for a tall window where the old man's workbench was. As soon as they stepped in at the door they saw that he had a customer, so the children turned to look at the rows of carved bears and goats, cows and chamois, which crowded tier upon tier of shelves.

Larger bears holding branches for hatstands, and jars for ferns, seemed to look at them out of the dark corners.

Grandmother went slowly forward towards a high wooden stool which stood beside a lathe. "Why! It is Madame!" exclaimed the woodcarver as he saw her, and his customer turned towards them. It was Helga.

They were all so surprised to see her that they almost forgot what they had come for. "Did you come on the boat? We didn't see you," cried Philippa.

"We saw Kati—she was with the school." Simon thought that Helga had been crying, and so did Grandmother, who said quickly, "We will go out and sit on the bench in the sun for a little while, and leave you to do your business, Helga. Then we want to choose some bears."

"It is no matter, Madame," said Helga, "for everyone knows my business. The whole world knows about last night it seems."

Out of the basket that she carried she lifted the three pieces of Mr. Berg's famous market, and some small turrets, and pieces of the houses which had snapped off. Old Mr. Hofner held up his hands in horror. He spoke hardly any English, but there was no doubt about what he thought.

He took the damaged pieces to his bench, and stood peering at them, rubbing a stubby finger into their dusty niches. Simon felt horribly sad, and ashamed too, as though he had broken the beautiful thing himself.

"So old Dani let you bring the carving here hoping it may be mended," said Grandmother, looking with sympathy at Helga's anxious face, "If anyone can do that Gerard Hofner can—at least Mr. Berg would not have lost it entirely."

It seemed a long time before the old man took off his spectacles, polished them on a check duster, and came to give his verdict. Simon and Philippa could only guess what he said, but they saw Grandmother's face brighten, and even Helga began to smile.

"Can he do it? Can he put it together?" whispered Philippa, giving Helga's sleeve a little tug.

"Almost as good as new," they were told. "To look at, at any rate. He will use strong contact glue for the big pieces that fit, and he will carve new little pieces and colour them to make them look like the old polished wood. Hans Uli will be happy."

Simon felt as though he could shout with joy, and Philippa ran to look at the bears again, in case Grandmother should forget them altogether.

"If only Hans Uli can be mended too," she thought, and

then gave all her attention to the enchanting little animals.

When they all went down to the boat together the children each carried their chosen treasure—a beautiful chamois on a steep little piece of rock for Philippa, and a bear with her cubs for Simon.

"I'd grow out of a pair of braces with flowers on them," he said, "but I'll never grow out of this."

"Why didn't we see you on the boat when we were coming?" Philippa asked Helga again as they went on board.

"I was with my friend who serves the lemonade. I have seen you, and Kati also, but I am not good company when I am sad, so I have stayed in the shadow."

"But you're not sad now that Mr. Berg's market can be mended," declared Simon, as they found their seats.

"A little less perhaps, but not happy till my father is home, and till I know if Hans Uli—if Hans Uli . . ." the tears were very near again, and Philippa caught Grandmother's eye. She gave Simon a push, and steered him to the other side of the boat.

"Come over here till we start," she said, "when people cry I don't know what to do."

They thought that the sail home was going to be rather tame after the novelty of the journey out. To begin with, Helga had told them that the school would not come on board again. A motorbus was to take them round by road after they had climbed through the forest, and that, thought Simon, would have been a perfect way of going home.

Grandmother gave them some francs to buy lemonade, and they took the short fat bottles to rest on the rail while they sucked their straws. It was still very hot, and they watched the ripples that the boat made in the calm water as she went on her quiet way. Philippa had just thought that it was rather like being in a dream, when the unexpected happened. A puff of wind lifted the limp Swiss flags on their short mast and sent some biscuit wrappers skidding down the deck. Then, with a violence they could never have imagined, a squall struck them. It seemed to rush across the great lake like a wall of air, whipping up waves till there were creamy caps of foam as far as they could see.

"It's a storm!" cried Simon. "It's a smashing storm! We're really going up and down—it's as good as the sea."

"It's horrible!" cried Philippa. "If the waves get bigger and bigger we might sink—I wish I was in that bus with Kati."

She made her way unsteadily to Grandmother, hampered by other passengers who were hurrying to the saloon for shelter from the wind.

"Will we sink, Grandma?" she asked, breathlessly, as some newspapers and a sunhat blew past them, and went over the rail into the foaming water.

Grandmother drew her down on to the seat, and held her close.

"I think not," she said placidly, "it's just a blow. It will be almost more noisy than this up in the forest, with the trees roaring."

Helga reached out and took Philippa's hand in her warm one. "Not to be frightened," she said, "one minute it is calm, and then storm—it is always so among the mountains. I think of the lake of Galilee—you will know that story?"

"When Jesus told the storm to be quiet," said Philippa, looking up from Grandmother's encircling arm, "Will He tell this one to be quiet too?"

"Soon, I think," said Helga, "but not perhaps till we are home."

She was silent again, and Philippa watched her pale face as she looked out across the wind tossed water. "Troubles are like storms," she thought, "before yesterday we were all happy. and then everything went nasty at once." She rested her head in the crook of Grandmother's arm, and in her heart she said a prayer that Jesus would help with Helga's troubles and Hans Uli's and poor Klaus Werner's.

"And even the old professor's, because he's upset at losing things," she added, and found suddenly that she was not afraid any more.

"I'm going out there with Simon," she said, "I want to watch those waves breaking up the rocks. They're almost getting the forest wet."

Several Surprises

9

THE WIND DROPPED AS SUDDENLY AS IT
had risen, and it was calm and still by the time they reached
their hotel again. Grandmother had insisted that Helga
should come with them in the taxi, and as she said 'Thank
you Madame for your kindness', and turned to go, Simon
called after her:

"I'm coming to turn the hay and feed the rabbits in a
little while, Grandmother says I can."

"Says we can" insisted Philippa, and ran off to show
Madame Rähmi the precious chamois.

Because the wind had dropped it seemed hotter than ever,
and they didn't run all the way to the chalet as usual.
Kati had just come back when they got there, her satchel
was full of pine cones, and she declared that she was starving.

She seemed to have forgotten that she had been shy on
the boat, and ran upstairs to find Helga, and tell her about
the picnic. Simon and Philippa wandered round the rabbit
hutches, and spent a long time feeding and petting each one.

"I s'pose we'd better rake that hay," said Simon, rather
half-heartedly because he was feeling hot and sticky. Even
the bees, humming round the blue tassels of blossom on the
balcony seemed lazier than usual.

Kati came down and joined them as they fetched the
rakes and began tossing and turning. "Helga goes to
the hospital to see Hans Uli," she said, "she is glad you are
here."

She found a fork and joined them, and for a few minutes
they worked properly. Then Kati started throwing hay in
all directions, and Philippa joined in. Simon threw down his
rake and ran to gather an armful with which to smother

72

them, but suddenly he remembered something. "If you trample it you will make bad hay," Helga had said on that very first afternoon. Making bad hay wouldn't help anyone.

"Hi! you girls," he shouted, "work properly—I'm boss around here tonight."

"Who said you were boss?" Philippa pushed a handful down his neck, and Kati began chanting something in German which he guessed was rude.

"Get on with it!" he commanded, though he was really longing to retaliate. "Get on with doing it properly, or we'll make bad hay."

He went to pick up his own rake, and was drawing some up to make into a haycock again, when the garden gate clicked. A slim, dark-haired man, with a very brown face, came into the yard. Simon stopped raking and wondered who he was, but Kati flew into his arms. Klaus Werner had come home.

"Only for a little while," he told them, rather sadly, when he had finished kissing Kati, and then he asked where Helga was.

"She's gone to the hospital," said Philippa, "she won't be back for ages I should think."

"I too am on my way there. I am glad you make the hay—I thank you, it is a help."

"And we've fed the rabbits," said Simon proudly, but Mr. Werner wasn't listening. He was looking up at the mountains, and the children turned and looked too. Grey wisps of cloud were coming across them, and the peaks were lost in mist.

"It will rain tonight, the hay should be indoors." Klaus Werner frowned and looked at his watch. "I need to be quick to the hospital," he said, and then glanced anxiously at the sky.

"We'll do it!" cried Simon. "We'll put it wherever you say, and we'll do it properly, truly we will."

"That is good—that is kind. Kati will show you."

Hans Werner quite cheered up for a moment, as he kissed Kati and turned to go.

"Tell Hans Uli we hope he's better, and tell him we were on the lake today," said Philippa, rocking about on her hay rake, and then she added, "Have they found the old Professor's papers? Is that why you could come home?"

Klaus Werner started, and drew in his breath sharply. "So you know about that," he said, with a touch of bitterness. "No, nothing is found, but much questioning has been done, and there will be more I think."

"Everybody knows," said Philippa, "it was on the radio, so everybody wants to know."

"And everybody has many strange ideas," said Mr. Werner, sadly, and went without another word.

"What did you want to say that for, you donkey," exclaimed Simon, fiercely. "It's none of your business."

"It's everybody's business—when it's on the radio," Philippa declared stubbornly, but all the same she wished she had never asked the question. Kati looked at them with a puzzled expression. She obviously didn't understand all they were saying, and she couldn't put her own thoughts into English, but she knew that somehow Philippa had made her father sad, and she turned and ran into the house. Suddenly the sun disappeared behind the grey clouds, and it was chilly.

"C'mon," said Simon gloomily, "we'd better get this job done, we said we would." They began drawing the hay into a pile, but Philippa had to go into the house and find Kati, because she would know where it had to go.

She came at last, unwillingly, and tugged open the door of a shed at the back of the chalet. "Here," she said, "it all goes here—if we push."

They went to and from with their arms full of it. They were sticky and dirty, with tickly pieces down inside their clothes before the job was finished, but Kati had cheered up, and the great pile inside the shed smelled wonderful.

They did have to give the last lot a push before they could close the door, and just as Simon did so the great drops began to fall.

"Just in time!" he panted, and they scampered for the balcony.

"We'd better go home," Philippa decided, going to look at the cuckoo clock. "We're so dirty that it won't matter getting wet as well."

"I go to Madame Knoble," said Kati, "Helga will know, I go always if she is not here."

Simon and Philippa were both very tired as well as being very wet and dirty by the time they presented themselves to Grandmother in her little sitting-room.

"Baths at once!" she exclaimed. "Madame Rähmi will say you are a disgrace to the hotel."

"But we were helping," Philippa protested. "Helga's father was pleased."

"Klaus Werner? Is he home?" Grandmother looked surprised and relieved as well.

"Only for a little," Simon told her, "he said there would be more questions. He went to the hospital, and we did the hay. Philippa was a fathead and asked him about those missing papers, and he looked awfully unhappy."

Grandmother frowned. "That was a bit blunt," she agreed. "If they are not found yet he must feel very uncomfortable. I know we are quite sure that he would not do anything wrong, but other people may think differently. I imagine that everyone who works at the Professor's chalet must be suspect. Even if nothing is discovered they might think that Mr. Werner gave secrets away, especially if the inventions are suddenly used in another country. I'm afraid he might even lose his job, if things aren't sorted out soon."

"Because the Professor wouldn't trust him any more?" asked Philippa sadly.

Grandmother nodded. "If that happened, nobody would trust him, and it might be hard for him to find work," she said. "It's a terrible thing not to be trusted, even if a person knows that he's innocent."

"I'm sorry I said that about the papers—I didn't mean to hurt him," muttered Philippa, and Simon drifted off towards the bathroom feeling that things had turned all grey, like the weather.

It rained steadily all the next day, and although Philippa was happy, learning how to knit, and doing games with Grandmother, Simon roamed about, restless and bored. He was delighted when Peter found time to teach him to make a chalet out of empty matchboxes, and even more pleased when the telephone rang, and Peter took a message to Grandmother from Helga.

"Hans Uli is home," he said, beaming. "He lies on his bed, of course, for many weeks I think, but if he is still it is good. Helga says he must go back again for X-rays, but he will run again before the winter."

"Wonderful news!" cried Grandmother, "I think it is an answer to many prayers, Peter. It's kind of Helga to tell us so quickly, she knows we are concerned, especially as Simon was mixed up in the affair."

"Tomorrow perhaps Hans Uli will like to see Simon, Helga has said so . . . " Peter gave this piece of news with his face creased into one of its biggest smiles, and Simon nearly ruined his matchbox chalet, sweeping it off the table in his excitement.

It rained most of the following day, and when Simon ran down the street, to buy some stamps for Grandmother, the mountains were quite hidden by grey clouds. But suddenly, in the afternoon, the clouds rolled away and the sun came out. When, later, he went off to see Hans Uli the sky was blue again, the cobbles were drying, and the wooden balconies and fences were steaming with the returning warmth.

Simon carried some grapes, and a box of modelling clay he had chosen at the shop beside the Post Office. Grandmother had told him that he must be very quiet, so he went up the stairway on tiptoe, but Helga came to meet him smiling.

"Hans Uli is awake," she said. "His head aches still a good deal, but he is lonely. When you should come away I will tell you."

So Simon went eagerly into the bare little bedroom, which had the curtain drawn to keep the light from Hans Uli's eyes. "Hullo!" he said, "I've come—and Grandma sends her love—and Philippa . . . "

Hans Uli interrupted him. "Shut the door! Something I must ask you before Helga comes."

"I'm not to make your head ache," Simon warned him, but Hans Uli sounded very wideawake. "My head is no matter," he said, "Tell me—what happened to Mr. Berg's market? Is it safe? I do not know except that I was falling, and when I speak of the stable to Helga she is cross, so I will not ask her . . . "

"It was broken," Simon told him sadly, "it was in three big pieces and lots of little bits. But the woodcarver down the lake has it now, he's going to make it as good as new—nearly—I don't think Mr. Berg will be too cross, I guess Helga was going to tell you after it was mended."

Hans Uli lay quite still except for his brown fingers restlessly twisting the edge of his bedcover. "Poor Mr. Berg," he said at last, "I am sad because I have done it. That woodcarver is the best in the Canton, but he cannot make it new."

"It's a pity about your photograph . . . " Simon didn't know quite what to say, and for once wished that Philippa was there. She would have been talking without a stop.

"The competition!" Hans Uli suddenly sounded interested. "There will not be school for me for a lot of days I think," he said, "but there is still time for a photograph. My camera can take things close—at the end of the bed—or on a table. From the window there is light enough. Only there is to think of something special that I could do better than Johannes."

"I'll find you something," said Simon at once, "I'll look tomorrow. Philippa will, too, and even Peter might think of something."

"Tomorrow!" exclaimed Hans Uli, rebelliously, "tomorrow I shall be flat like this, and many tomorrows the doctor says. Always I am so unfortunate. Is the sun out?"

Simon went to the window and held the curtain back. "It's out bright, the rain's all gone. We got the hay into the shed before it came. Did Helga tell you?"

There was no answer, just a muffled sound from the bed which made Simon turn swiftly. With the coverlet pulled up over his face, Hans Uli was crying.

"Don't!" urged Simon in a panic. "Oh, please, don't do that! Helga will be cross—she'll say I upset you!"

"It is I who upset," gulped Hans Uli, "I am lazy and I make trouble—I think God will make me to lie like this because I am bad, and because I would not think about Him! Now I am punished, and my father is still in trouble."

"But God won't make you lie like that," cried Simon. "Peter told us you would run before the winter. You fell because you were silly to stand on that old barrow, but we've all been saying our prayers for you, and God has let you be well enough to come home. You jolly well ought to say 'thank You' to Him for that! You tell Him you're sorry for being lazy and stupid, and then start all over again. He'll forgive you, and help you, I know He will—and I guess it's someone else being bad that's made trouble for your father. Listen!" he added earnestly, "Jesus died so that everyone can be forgiven if they are sorry—you believe that don't you? Well, ask Him to help you!"

Hans Uli let the coverlet fall, and looked hard at Simon with his big grey eyes. "You and Philippa feel God is near, like Helga does" he said with a sniff, "I wish I could, but I don't know how to start."

Simon sat on the edge of the bed and thought very hard.

"I guess you start by saying you're sorry," he said, "and then by saying 'thank You' for everything—the sun, and the sky, and what you eat, and because the rabbits are so soft to touch. Then, somehow, you'll know He's there, and everything will seem twice as nice."

In the room beyond the cuckoo clock called five times, and they heard Helga coming along the balcony. "Time to let Hans Uli rest now," she said, pushing the curtain aside, and looking in.

Simon slid off the bed. "I'll come tomorrow," he promised, "when we've looked very hard for something special."

"While you look for it I will be thinking," said Hans Uli soberly, then, with a sudden smile he added, "and saying thank You'!"

The Shining Peaks

10 SIMON WAS STILL THINKING ABOUT HANS
Uli when he sat down to breakfast next morning, and was
sad because he would not be out in the sun, but something
happened a few moments later which made him forget
everything else.

"This is your big day, Simon," Grandmother said,
offering him a roll, and pushing cherry jam in his direction.
She had a letter propped against the coffee pot, and Philippa
was making the envelope into a boat.

"What sort of big day?" begged Simon. "You might
hurry up and tell me."

"A little suspense is good for you," Grandmother told
him, but her eyes were smiling. "Two great friends of mine
are coming through the town today. I think I mentioned
them before—Captain and Mrs. Yates. When he's not in
charge of a big liner on the high seas Captain Yates loves
the mountains, and they are going to drive up quite high
today, and take a picnic. They have asked you to go too . . . "

Simon gave such a shout of joy that everyone in the hotel
dining room looked round.

"S-hussh! Don't knock the coffee over. You're a big boy,
just see that you're a sensible one too." Grandmother took
the jam away from his elbow, and Simon pushed his
plate away as well. He was far too excited to eat. "Can't
Philippa come too?" he asked, realising that she had not
been mentioned.

"I don't want to come," Philippa said quickly. "Grandmother asked me before you came down, but it's too high—
I'd rather be here."

"You said you'd climb higher than me once," Simon reminded her.

"That was before the green mountain," she said.

After breakfast Simon fidgetted about in and out of the yard, watching for the car to come. He was enormously excited, and Philippa was happy because later in the day Grandmother was taking her to buy the Swiss blouse that she wanted so much at the embroidery shop. She had planned to fill in the blank morning by visiting Hans Uli while Simon was away.

At last a dark green car slid to a stop, and a tall, grey-haired man got out. A sprightly little lady followed him, and Simon liked her at once. She had a very sun-tanned face, and looked just the right sort of person to have a picnic with.

Grandmother came slowly out to meet them, but to Simon's joy they didn't stay long talking. Soon he was in the back of the car, with a bulging rucksack and some sturdy shoes stowed beside them. He felt a very important person as they waved good-bye, and drove off down the sunny street.

It was not till they were nearly out in the country that Simon remembered he had promised to spend the day looking for something which would make a good photograph—something small enough to put at the end of Hans Uli's bed. Because of all the excitement it had been quite forgotten.

"Perhaps we'll stop at a village where I could buy something for him," he thought, feeling guilty, and was glad that Grandmother had given him some pocket-money. But try as he would, he couldn't think what he might see in a shop which would be really 'special'. After a while he gave up trying and looked at the lovely countryside.

"We shall be having our picnic up among the snow," said Mrs. Yates, turning round to smile at him, "and later on we shall probably walk in the forest. Look out now, and see all you can. Switzerland is so wonderful in May that you don't want to miss anything."

Simon was quite glad that they didn't want to talk to him much after that. He was absorbed in the beauty of the flower-starred fields, the scattered farms, the apple trees laden with blossom, and the cream-coloured cows which swung their bells as they moved slowly in the sunshine.

He wanted to shout with excitement as they drove beside rivers which came foaming down from the hills, swirling round jagged rocks. There were waterfalls, too, as the road climbed higher, plumes of shining water and spray which fell from immense heights into the green valleys.

All the time the white peaks grew nearer, and nearer, till at last Captain Yates stopped the car at a village which nestled amongst them. It was built on steep slopes, the alpine meadows and forests of fir trees rose high above it on one side, and on the other a gigantic mountain range towered into the sky.

Simon got out of the car and stood gazing upwards. The sun was so bright, and the air so still, that it was very hot.

"Put on your anorak," said Captain Yates, fetching his own from the back seat, "we're going to need them for a little while—you'll be surprised."

And Simon was, enormously surprised. The Captain shouldered the rucksack, and the three of them walked up a little lane and into a small green meadow. Just beyond the gate there was a shed which Simon thought was a barn, but Mrs. Yates called "Hurry! We're just in time for the last chair lift before it stops for lunch."

"Chair lift? What's a chair lift?" began Simon, but the Captain hustled him into the shed. "You'd better come with me" he said. "My wife can go with that other lady."

Simon was rapidly enveloped in an enormous brown mackintosh lined with felt, which a man in uniform tucked round him, while the grown-ups struggled into theirs. Then, as a curious little swinging seat came rumbling into the shed, he was picked up, and firmly pushed into it. A steel bar locked across in front of him, and Captain Yates said "Here we go!"

With a sudden rush the little chair on its tough steel cable shot out at the back of the shed and into the sunshine. For a moment the ground was close below them, and then it dropped away. Their pace slowed, and silently they began to float upwards.

Simon had a feeling that he must be dreaming. They could see the chair that Mrs. Yates was in swinging some way beyond them on the cable, but otherwise they seemed to be alone in the world.

Soon they passed over a little farm, just above its rooftops, but except for the tinkle of the cowbells it seemed deserted. Simon realised with amazement that the toy village in the valley, far, far below, was the one they had just left.

"Enjoying it old fellow?" Captain Yates looked down at him kindly and seemed pleased when Simon answered, "It's too nice to talk."

"If one talks one can't listen," agreed the Captain, and listening Simon heard a church bell ringing somewhere, and a cuckoo calling across the steep little fields. "What's that funny noise?" he asked, looking down, and cried out with pleasure at the mass of flowers just below him.

"Crickets chirping—they do it all the time. Do you see the gentians? That vivid blue—and white and pink campion, and great big forget-me-nots."

"And cowslips and buttercups together—and something purple!" cried Simon, "It's like the hundreds and thousands Mother puts on party cakes. Are there any edelweiss like Hans Uli has on his jacket?"

"Not here I think, they're even higher up than this, right at the edge of the snow, but you'll see wild cyclamen a little further on."

They were silent again as they swung up through a scented fir forest, and then Simon suddenly shivered. A cold breath of air came down from above and Captain Yates leaned over to tuck his wrap round him.

"Can you feel the snow chill? We're nearly there."

Soon there were no trees and flowers beneath them, but brown peaty looking earth, and big rocks with patches of snow scattered among them. Two minutes later there was no brown to be seen, but a white, dazzling snow field all round, and the white mountains so close on every side.

"We're here!" said the Captain, and the chair slid to a stop under the high roof. They had left the everyday world seven thousand feet below.

Mrs. Yates was being helped out of her chair just as they arrived.

"That was great, wasn't it?" she asked. "Are you hungry!"

"I'm starving!" cried Simon, suddenly remembering that he had been too excited to eat his breakfast.

They went up some steps and out on to a broad platform, which hung like a huge balcony over the snowy slopes. The platform was crowded with people all eating packed lunches at long wooden tables, and drinking hot coffee bought from the cafe alongside.

"Run and take that corner table," Mrs. Yates told Simon, "be quick—there are some hikers heading that way."

Simon dived between the crowded benches and slid into a seat right at the edge of the balcony. It felt hot as he touched it, and he peeled off his anorak. Everyone else was doing the same. Now that they were not swinging in the air he could not feel the snow chill at all.

It was the best meal he had ever eaten in his life, he decided, as they unpacked the rolls and eggs, sausages and lettuce. He rather wished that Philippa had been with him, but Hans Uli would have been better. It was thinking of Hans Uli that made him remember the edelweiss. Captain Yates had said that it grew up near the snow. If only he could find just one tiny bunch to take back with him!

He sat drumming his heels against the wooden bench, and

thinking how special those alpine flowers were. If Hans Uli had some in a vase by his bed perhaps he could photograph them in all their lovely colour. He had that extra gadget which helped him to take things that were very close. If he did that he could put something good in the exhibition after all.

Simon remembered with joy that Mrs. Yates had said that they might go for a walk presently. She was talking to her husband at that moment, and they were both watching some climbers on the white crags opposite them.

"Do you want to stretch your legs a bit my boy?" asked the Captain, suddenly remembering that he was there, and moved so that Simon could slide out of the seat.

"You'll get a different view from the other side," Mrs. Yates told him. "We shall be here for half an hour yet, and you know where to find us."

Gladly Simon made his way along the platform, leaving them gazing through the field-glasses. It was good to be on his own for a while. He looked inside the cafe, watched some climbers heaving on their heavy packs, and drifted round to the other side of the balcony. It was cold on that side in the shade, but his heart gave a little jump of excitement. Two young men were walking out across the snow, right to the edge of that shining slope.

A moment later Simon had wriggled under the rails, and dropped the short distance to a powdery little drift.

A Gift for Hans Uli

11

SIMON PICKED HIMSELF UP AND LOOKED around. The snow close to him was hard and firm, in spite of the sun, and perhaps if he walked to the edge of it he would find the edelweiss there, waiting for him. He dusted the dry snow off himself, and set off, going gingerly at first, and then with confidence.

He stopped a moment when he had gone a little distance, and stood looking across at the enormous snowy range beyond, and the deep purple shadows on those frozen heights. He was right up among them at last, and Grandmother had said it would be a great day for him. It was more splendid that he could ever have imagined.

When he turned round again the young men were out of sight. Simon went on, following their line of footprints for some way, and then striking off on a path of his own. The slope was not too steep, and soon he saw some patches of brown earth beyond him. With a thrill of excitement he began to run.

That was his undoing. He had not realised that he was so near the edge of a sheer cliff of rock, or that the brown earth was still partly frozen. Suddenly his feet shot from under him, and he fell heavily.

The next moment he was rolling helplessly. He was too terrified even to scream as he went over the edge, or when he plunged into a snowdrift twelve feet below. Unfortunately there were rocks sticking up through that drift, and Simon banged his head on one, and bruised his leg badly on another. It was icy cold too, because the deep drift was in the shade, and his anorak was away up there on the seat beside Mrs. Yates.

Luckily the snowdrift was only a patch, caught among the rocks, and beyond it there was a stretch of vivid colour. Grass and flowers flourishing together where nothing shaded them from the sun.

When Simon tried to struggle to his feet he gave a sharp yelp of pain and fell sideways. His left leg was far too uncomfortable to stand on. He tried again, because he simply must get out into the warm sunshine, and found it much easier to flounder along on all fours. It was difficult even to do that on the bumpy ground, and his leg hurt terribly.

At last he made his way to a sunny patch and sat there. Perhaps the pain, and a nasty headache, would go off a bit, he thought, if he stayed still and got warm. He wondered how soon Captain Yates would come looking for him, because he was quite certain he could never climb up that rocky cliff by himself. He knew, too, that he had done a very stupid thing, and hoped very much that the Captain would not be too furious with him.

"But at least I can get some flowers for Hans Uli—real alpine ones," he thought, to cheer himself up. He began to gather all he could reach, hardly needing to move at all. Yellow blooms, and white, blue and delicate pink, flowers whose names he did not know, and he just hoped that one of them was edelweiss, because he couldn't quite remember the shape of the ones on those black jackets.

He was beginning to feel better, and wished that Philippa was there to see all that blossom. "I'll get plenty of each kind," he thought, "and then Grandmother can have some." He wriggled determinedly for several yards with only an agonised yelp now and then when his leg twisted. Seeing a patch of vivid purple colour he edged towards it, and it was then that he saw the haversack.

It was a very old, shabby haversack, lying wedged between two rocks with a broken strap trailing on the ground. Simon lifted it on to his knees and turned it over. "Somebody's dropped a picnic—poor them," he thought. The lettesr A.S. were painted on the flap, and almost worn away with much use. It felt very light for a picnic he decided, and opened it out of curiosity.

He was very disappointed with the contents. Just a pink folder like his father had on his desk at home, and a stiff packet done up in polythene.

"That could be some sort of sandwiches," he decided, and wondered if a climber had left it between the rocks because the shoulder strap had broken, and would be fetching it as he came down. He was just going to put it back as he found it, when a sound from above caught his attention. Looking up he realised for the first time that the cable of the chair lift was right above him. A moment later a chair swung into view. The lunch time was over.

Wincing with pain Simon struggled to his feet and shouted. If only someone in a chair would notice him, perhaps they could get a message to Captain Yates by some people coming up. The shadow of the swinging travellers passed over him, and he yelled again. A surprised face peered down, and a young woman waved cheerfully before she sank out of sight below the edge of the distant rocks.

Simon almost cried. "They must think I'm just a Swiss boy shouting a greeting," he decided, and suddenly the mountain felt very, very lonely.

"But I'm not alone really," he remembered, after a minute. "I know I'm not alone because God is always near me. He knows I've been awfully silly, but He won't leave me all by myself."

The thought was very comforting. The sudden remembrance that God had made those majestic mountains as well as the fragile flowers he had picked made him feel curiously humble, but very happy.

"Please let somebody come and find me soon," he said aloud, "and please let Hans Uli know that You are near him when he sees wonderful things like this."

Although he was beginning to feel much better, Simon wished very much that he had his anorak. A few minutes ago he had been quite warm in the sun, but now wisps of mist were folding round the high peaks beyond him, and he shivered. Another chair swung overhead, and another, and another, but each time the passengers just waved cheerfully. A boy with his picnic lunch beside him, they thought, seeing the brown haversack, and the bunch of flowers he had gathered. "And perhaps lots of them don't understand English," he reasoned, wishing desperately that Captain Yates would come.

But at last someone took notice. "I've hurt my leg!" Simon shouted to a girl and a boy who leaned out from each side of their chair.

"Right! We'll get help . . . " the boy yelled back before they disappeared.

Thankfully Simon sat back and waited, and after what seemed a long. long time he heard Captain Yates calling his name. He looked up and saw him peering down from the top of the rocks. "Stay where you are," called the Captain, "I'll have to find a way round to you. It's no good me getting down if you can't get up. Just sit and wait. I shan't be long."

It took a little time to find a safe way to reach the level place where Simon was, but when at last the Captain appeared he had brought someone with him, a sturdy Swiss, whom he called Joseph.

"What on earth made you do such an idiotic thing as to go off by yourself?" he asked angrily as he tramped across the turf towards Simon. "We hunted all round the place for you, and my wife was getting frantic. I'm glad some young people telephoned the cafe to say a boy was hurt. We thought you had more sense."

He broke off suddenly. "What's this?" he demanded, picking up the haversack.

"It was here," muttered Simon, who was feeling very

much ashamed. "I found it between two rocks—it was stuck—there's nothing much in it, I guess it's someone's picnic." At that moment Joseph picked him up. "Hold tight!" he said, and Simon thankfully clutched his green jacket.

The pain, as his leg hung down, made his head swim, and he just hoped that Joseph wouldn't drop him. They set off along a tiny level track below the rocks, but for a moment Captain Yates didn't follow. He had pulled out the pink folder from the haversack, and torn back the polythene from the packet. As he opened it he gave a long, astonished whistle.

A minute later he caught the others up. "Can you manage by yourself?" he asked Joseph. "I have an urgent phone call to make."

"We go steady, no need for help," Joseph assured him, and Captain Yates passed them with caution, before scrambling ahead at a tremendous speed. In a few minutes he was out of sight, and Simon leaned his head on Joseph's shoulder, trying not to wince or cry when he was jolted. The stalwart Swiss lifted him over boulders, and got him up awkward slopes with amazing agility.

When at last he was set down gently on a chair in the cafe Mrs. Yates hastened to wrap his anorak round his shoulders, and added her own as well. To his relief she was not cross, she was even smiling.

"I'm not going to scold you," she said, "though you did make us very anxious indeed. It was a very thoughtless, silly thing you did, but I'm sure you've learned your lesson, and we think you have found something wonderful which a great many people have been looking for."

Simon was feeling rather sick at that moment, so he hardly took in what she said. "Can we go home soon?" he asked, "I got these flowers for Hans Uli, and I do hurt a lot."

"We'll have to wait a few minutes. There's a hot coffee

coming for you," Mrs. Yates told him comfortingly, "I guess that bang on the head hasn't helped. You've got a lump as big as an egg."

But they didn't have to wait long. Simon was still drinking the coffee when a tall man in a grey uniform arrived. A wide grey cloak hung from his shoulders, and Captain Yates began talking to him in German, both of them looking very excited and pleased. To Simon's dismay they said nothing about going home, but went down some steps from the platform, and strode out across the snow.

"Don't worry," Mrs. Yates told him, "that's a Swiss policeman. He wants to see exactly where you fell."

Ten minutes later she and Simon were tucked into a chair, and she leaned across and put her arm round him to hold him close. "Soon down now—shut your eyes," she suggested, and to his own surprise Simon was glad to do just that.

Captain Yates carried him to the police car which awaited them at the bottom, and the tall policeman with the cloak carried the haversack. He looked at Simon with a broad smile. "Very good boy!" he said.

It was only then that a wonderful idea occurred to Simon. "That's not what the Professor lost is it? Is it?" he asked eagerly. "How did it get there? I thought it was a picnic!"

"Well we're not certain, but we think that folder is the cause of all the trouble," said Mrs. Yates. "If it is, it's a jolly good thing that you went for that silly walk."

Smoothly the big car drove away, up roads with hairpin bends, and quite alarming views of other roads far below. At last they turned into a paved yard beside a chalet. It was so covered with flowers that the balconies looked like shadowy caves.

"We get out here," Captain Yates told Simon. "Just answer Professor Stahel clearly if he asks you questions. Tell him exactly what you did when you went for that walk, and if you saw anyone."

"Only people in the chairs going down, and the boy I called to," said Simon, feeling very excited. He was helped into a big, cool room, and an immensely fat man, with thick curly hair, came hurrying in. He evidently knew Mrs. Yates well, and with great delight shook hands with her.

"I am greatly indebted to you and your good husband," he kept saying, but Mrs. Yates turned to Simon, who had been put into a vast armchair.

"This is the young man who found your property," she said. "I think that perhaps the whole world will be indebted to him."

Professor Stahel balanced himself on the chair arm and looked down at Simon. "Did you realise, my boy, that those papers were the precious ones which had been stolen from me?" he asked.

In spite of his aching head Simon sat up straight.

"I didn't guess then—I thought it was a picnic, but the policeman and Captain Yates were so pleased that Mrs. Yates guessed they must be pretty special. Are they really the ones that there was something on the radio about? Will they really help space men some day?"

"Airmen certainly, and perhaps spacemen, and a lot of people on this beautiful earth I hope," the Professor told him, and then, because he said that Simon had a right to know, he explained a lot of things carefully.

"It seems that there are some people, probably in another country, who would like to take my hard work and use it for themselves," he said. "They could make a lot of money by selling what has taken me years to discover, and perhaps it would not be used for helping, and healing as I intended. I was very sad, too, because those big policemen thought that my good friend Klaus Werner might have something to do with it. He drives my car, you see, Simon, and he could go to Basle perhaps, while I was busy, and I would not know. Of course I was certain that he would not sell my secrets to anyone, but these policemen—they have funny ideas!"

The Professor smiled across at the tall man in grey, who smiled back, and didn't seem to mind in the least.

"But who did take it?" Simon asked, "And why was your secret in the haversack?"

"We do not know yet, but I think possibly a young man who passed as a student climbing among the mountains. One such has been seen near this chalet a great deal lately. He spent much time resting in the meadow across the road. I think he must have climbed the balcony the other day and helped himself to my work while I had breakfast. We all have breakfast on the far side of the house. He helped himself to my haversack, too, and walked out again. He was clever. When I discovered my papers were gone, then the village was full of policemen. But they asked about cars, you understand—about getting away quickly."

"And he had gone up in the chair lift!" exclaimed Captain Yates, "Just mixed with the holiday people, and dropped the haversack on the way up."

"Exactly! He came down carrying nothing. He knew just where to find it again when he was ready. He knew it would be waterproof, my good old haversack." The Professor got up, and went across to speak to the policeman. "I am truly glad that my old friend Klaus Werner cannot be connected with the affair any more," he said. "You see, that haversack hung on a hook in my study. I saw it before I went to breakfast, and Klaus came with me to speak about the car while I ate. I had not worked with those papers for several days—they were put away in my desk. I had been to Paris—by train—so Klaus had been here alone. But I saw my haversack that morning, and it is the proof of his innocence."

"Hans Uli will be glad, and Helga will be very glad!" cried Simon, before the policeman could answer. "Helga was crying about it, and Hans Uli was so angry. He said he knew his father would not steal."

"Ah! Then you will not regret that big bump on your head, it has been for a good cause," Professor Stahel said kindly, but then he added with a slight frown, "You were picking wild flowers? I see you still have some. Visitors are asked not to pick the flowers from the alpine meadows you know, If everyone did, then there would soon be none for others to enjoy. We have so many visitors in the spring, and we want them to see the wonderful fields for years to come."

"But I wanted them for Hans Uli," explained Simon, looking sadly at the drooping little bunch he still held, and suddenly he felt that he must tell them all about it. About the Exhibition for schools, and how necessary it was for Hans Uli to photograph something special.

"And you see the swan went away, and the squirrel wouldn't stay" he said despondently, "and now Mr. Berg's carving is broken. It's being mended, but Hans Uli can't make a picture of it, and he does so want to win. I thought that alpine flowers could be put at the end of his bed." He looked round as he ended his story, wondering if they all understood just how important it was.

"So you thought you might find the edelweiss?" asked Alexis Stahel gently. "Well, one day perhaps you will. When you are a little older you shall come and stay with me. The edelweiss grows very high, but Klaus Werner shall take you climbing—with Hans Uli of course!"

Simon flushed to the roots of his hair with sheer joy, but before he could answer properly the Professor strode out of the room. He came back a moment or two later with the most wonderful carving that any of them had ever seen. Even the Swiss policeman was full of admiration.

From two tiny wooden milk pails grew a mass of delicate starry flowers, all cut from the same wood, and painted white by some craftsman long ago.

"There!" said the big man, balancing the beautiful things on his broad palm, "Now you have edelweiss that will not fade. One will be something very special for Hans Uli to photograph—it has more than a hundred years—what you call a 'museum piece'. It is to help him get better. The other is for you, to say 'thank you' for tumbling over my haversack."

The rest of the day passed like a dream for Simon. A wonderful tea was brought for them by a cheerful girl in a very gay apron, and Simon quite forgot he had been feeling sick when he saw the Swiss pastries. Then the Professor helped him out on to the balcony, and let him look through a big telescope down into the valley far below.

"The houses down there look so tiny, it's nearly like being in an aeroplane," he said, and thinking of aeroplanes made him remember that his holiday would soon be over. What a lot he would have to tell Mother and Father—he knew it would be lovely to see them again, and his own garden, and the woods beyond the stream.

At last Captain Yates came to tell him that it was time to go, and although he was very sorry to leave the lovely chalet, Simon realised that he was feeling very, very tired.

Quite a lot of people had gathered to wave him goodbye, for the word had gone round that the Professor's papers were found. He waved back shyly as he was helped into Captain Yates' car which had been brought up from the village and was waiting outside. Klaus Werner had driven it up, and he was smiling all over his face as he shook hands with Simon.

"Tomorrow I shall have a whole day at home," he said. "Hans Uli will be glad of it."

"Tell him I'll be coming to see him," said Simon eagerly, "I guess I can if my leg doesn't hurt too much—I've got to see him really, because I've got a present for him, and he and I have an enormous secret."

"That is a good thing!" Klaus Werner looked immensely pleased. "But you have given him the best gift already," he added, "because of your walk in the snow today he has no more worries about me I think."